GHOSTLY HAUNTS

Published in *association with*

The National Trust

·

GHOSTLY HAUNTS

EDITED BY MICHAEL MORPURGO

Illustrated by Nilesh Mistry

PAVILION

First published in Great Britain in 1994 by
PAVILION BOOKS LIMITED
26 Upper Ground, London SE1 9PD

Designed by Sara Robin

A CIP catalogue record for this book is available
from the British Library.

ISBN 1 85793 158 0

Printed in Hong Kong by Mandarin Offset

2 4 6 8 10 9 7 5 3 1

This book can be ordered direct from the publisher.
Please contact the Marketing Department.
But try your bookshop first.

THE NATIONAL TRUST 1895-1995
GHOSTLY HAUNTS

On 12 January 1895, the National Trust for Places of Historic Interest or Natural Beauty was founded by three far-sighted Victorians: Octavia Hill, who wanted 'open air sitting rooms' for poor city dwellers, Robert Hunter, a skilful lawyer, and Hardwicke Rawnsley, Vicar of St Margaret's at Wray in Windermere. Their first property for the Trust was four and a half acres of cliff on the Welsh coast.

One hundred years later the Trust has come a long way. Now Europe's most active conservation organization, it cares for over 300 historic houses, most of which are open to the public, 580,000 acres of countryside and 534 miles of coast. Wherever you are in England, Wales or Northern Ireland, you are not far from Trust land.

Many of these properties, and the animals that inhabit them, have inspired writers in the past. Even before the Trust was formed, the poet, William Wordsworth, declared that the Lake District should be 'a sort of national property' to which everyone who had an 'eye to perceive and a heart to enjoy' should have access. We could easily add 'a pen to describe' to his list of qualifications; Beatrix Potter, Rudyard Kipling, Kenneth Grahame, Virginia Woolf and Arthur Ransome, amongst many others, all wrote about National Trust land or lived in houses now cared for by the Trust. They have all loved and visited some National Trust place, and have returned to it in their minds – and with their pens – to capture it forever on paper.

In the Trust's centenary year it is therefore fitting that some of the best writers of today should, at Michael Morpurgo's invitation, turn to the Trust for inspiration for their new and spellbinding ghostly tales.

THE NATIONAL TRUST

A royalty from the sale of this book will go to the National Trust. By buying this book you are helping the Trust, an independent charity, to protect all the historic houses, gardens, coast and countryside it cares for throughout England, Wales and Northern Ireland.

For further information about the Trust, or any of its properties, contact The National Trust's Membership Department, P.O. Box 39, Bromley, Kent BR1 1NH.

CONTENTS

INTRODUCTION

 This introduction will be a story, a true story. That way you might actually stop to read it and not turn at once to the first of the 'Ghostly Haunts'.

Some twenty years ago, my wife Clare began an educational charity called Farms for City Children. The idea was to enable our city children to spend a week of the school year living and working on a farm. These 'acorns' of our future needed, she felt, fertile soil, sunshine and clean rain, if they were to grow tall and healthy. Such a week might help them a little, and maybe a lot.

For ten years or more, a thousand children a year came to Nethercott Farm near Iddesleigh, North Devon, the pioneer farm project. Demand proved to be so great that we began to look for another 'children's' farm.

Then I met a man in a pub, the Duke of York, Iddesleigh – the best pub in England, incidentally. He turned out to be Peter Mitchell, the National Trust Land Agent for South Wales (now the Regional Director). We got talking. He came to see what Farms for City Children did at Nethercott Farm. We went to see what the National Trust was doing in South Wales.

Peter Mitchell took us on a tour of National Trust properties in his area. I remember particularly the gold mine at Dolaucothi; and farms, lots of farms, one of which the National Trust had just acquired through its coastal fundraising project, Enterprise Neptune.

Perched dramatically on the Pembrokeshire coastal path, the place was wild and windswept. Surrounded by sea on three sides, the farm looked out towards Ramsey Island. Treginnis Isaf, or Lower Treginnis, was an eighteenth-century farmstead, derelict but still just intact. There was a wonderful dovecot in the farmyard, 300 rocky acres, golden gorse blazing in the sun, buzzards mewing and wheeling above us, seals bobbing in the coves, and porpoises far out to sea. At night we saw the badgers lurruping along the tracks and heard the foxes barking. We met the farmer who thought it was a fine idea to have a thousand city children a year on the farm. Honestly!

Four years on, and with the help of the National Trust, Farms for City Children completed a major renovation of the farm buildings, and Treginnis Isaf opened its doors to its first city child. They're there now, cleaning out sheds, helping with lambing, collecting eggs, driving the sheep, feeding the pigs and calves – farmers for a week. But not only farmers. Here they learn, too, of the giants who came across, thousands of years ago, from Ireland and hurled rocks at the Welsh giants – the rocks are still scattered all over the farm. They hear of pirates and wreckers. And they hear of the ghosts that haunt the copper mine on the farm, their plaintive cries echoing up the mineshafts on still, dark nights. Even the gulls won't go near the place. Shivery. Walking back from feeding the calves last thing at night, the children can feel the ghosts around them. They dream their dreams, paint their pictures, write their stories.

To celebrate the centenary of the National Trust, I asked some grown-up children, some of the very best, most magical authors of our time, to remember some National Trust place, some house or farm, some hill or valley, to revisit it in their minds, and then to dream their dreams and write their stories. Each responded in her or his inimitable way – Berlie Doherty from the darkness of a cottage in Dorset where we witness a birth; John Quinn from an island of ghosts, Coney Island in Lough Neagh, Northern Ireland; Dick King-Smith from any National Trust farm you like (so long as they have headless chickens). Anne Merrick goes through a mirror at Castle Drogo in Devon and we go with her; Joan Aiken takes us into some ancient, musty manor that could be almost anywhere – you can feel the cobwebs on your face; Alick Rowe listens to Elgar and writes his own enigmatic variation; Terence Blacker resurrects a bloated vampire in Norfolk; and Jamila Gavin's demon drummer will beat in your head long after you've finished reading about him. I myself managed to find a National Trust house that never was, that no one ever visited.

But we'll begin with Ted Hughes, Poet Laureate (and President of Farms for City Children) who takes us to the Yorkshire moors, the ghostly haunt of his childhood.

Michael Morpurgo

THE
DEADFALL

TED HUGHES

I own a tiny ivory fox about an inch and a half long. Most likely an Eskimo carving. It came to me in one of the strangest incidents of my life.

My mother saw ghosts, now and again. Different kinds. One night during the last war she woke, feeling dreadfully agitated. She lay for a while, feeling more and more agitated. At last she got out of bed and, opening the curtains, saw an amazing sight. Across the street stood St George's Church. And above the church, the whole sky was throbbing with flashing crosses. As she told of it next day, there were thousands on thousands, flashing and fading, in and out, the whole sky covered with them, coming very thick, like big snowflakes hitting and breaking and melting on a warm window. She tried to wake my father. 'There's the most terrible battle somewhere,' she told him. 'Thousands of boys are being killed.' He heard what she said, but he wouldn't be roused. He had to get up at five a.m. anyway, as every morning. She went back to the window and watched for a long time, going to bed finally only when she got too cold.

Next day, the radio announced that the British and American armies had landed that night in Northern France, and were fighting their way inland through the German defences.

Another time, she was awakened by a sickening pain across the back of her neck and a terrific banging. Short, urgent bursts of banging, as if somebody were pounding hard on a door or hammering on a table. She couldn't tell where the noise came from. 'It shook this house,' she said. Again she got up and looked out of the window. But the street, which was the main street of the town, was deserted. She went downstairs, made herself a cup of tea, and sat with the pain. It felt, she said, like toothache – but in her neck. She couldn't tell how the banging stopped – eventually it just wasn't there any more. But she still had the pain next morning when the telegram came with the news of the violent death, during the night, of one of her brothers.

She was ready for this news. She had known somebody in her family was going to die. And the moment she read the telegram the pain went.

Another time, while she was pushing a Hoover around the sitting room, mid-afternoon, her eldest brother walked in. She was alarmed, since she knew that he was actually lying unable to move in Halifax hospital. As she switched off the Hoover to speak to him, he faded. She noted the time, guessing he had died that very moment. Again, she had known that one of her family was going to die.

Each time, she was warned in the same way. Among her seven or eight brothers and sisters, as a girl her closest friend had been the sister closest to her in age, Miriam. This sister died when both were in their late teens. A few months after her death, Miriam reappeared at night and sat on my mother's bed, just as in life, and held her hand. Without speaking, she seemed to be consoling my mother. Two days later, their baby brother died.

After that, through the years, just before any member of her family died, Miriam would appear at my mother's bedside. But as the years passed, her ghost changed. She became brighter and taller. 'Gradually,' said my mother, 'she has turned into an angel.' By the time of that last occasion, when their eldest brother died, Miriam had become a tall glowing angel with folded wings. My mother described her as being made of flame. As if she were covered with many-coloured feathers of soft, pouring flame. But it was still Miriam. And on this last visit, as she stood by the bed, my mother reached up to stroke the flame because it was, as she said, 'so beautiful'. 'The feel of it,' she told us afterwards, 'was like the taste of honey.' I remember her telling that, the next day, as if it were minutes ago.

•

My brother and sister and I also wanted to see ghosts.

We lived near Hebden Bridge, in West Yorkshire, in a village called Mytholmroyd. There the river runs in a deep valley, under high horizons of empty moorland. On one side of that valley, in a steep wood of oak and birch trees, is an ancient grave. At least, it was always known as a grave. We called it the grave of the ancient Briton. A great rough slab of stone. My brother, much older than myself, sometimes tried to dig him up, with the help of a few friends. I remember scraping away there, on two or three occasions. The stone was embedded in a hole and far too big for us to lever out. We tried to dig round it and under it. But the great slab simply settled deeper.

My brother liked to camp out on the hillsides, and would take me with him. Once, when he and I were camping down by the stream in that wood, not far from the grave, he got the idea of raising the ancient Briton's ghost.

He must have already thought about it quite carefully, because he was prepared. Perhaps not very well prepared. He had brought half a bottle of sweet wine made from blackberries. One of our uncles concocted that sort of thing. This was to work the magic trick.

He woke me in the middle of the night. I pulled on my boots and climbed through the woods behind him. I liked being in the woods at night, but by the time we got to the grave I was nervous. I remember I didn't want him to go too near the grave. I thought something might grab him and pull him in. Then I would be alone, in a dark wood, with my brother somewhere beneath me being dragged deeper into the earth. I didn't like that idea.

He had already made what he called the altar – a flat piece of stone near the grave's edge. Now he lit a fire on this stone. I saw he had fire-wood ready. In his preparations he had even emptied the charge out of some twelve-bore cartridges, to make sure he got an instant flare-up blaze, by lighting the loose explosive. That bit was a success. It lit up the tree trunks and the over-curving boughs in a great woosh of light, as if they'd flung up their arms. Then it settled down to burn the twigs he'd piled in a wigwam shape. He was an expert firemaker and in no time had a good blaze going.

Now he stood up with his bottle of wine and carefully tipped it, letting a trickle spatter into the flames. The glow blackened and hissed, as a great cloud billowed up. He began to speak:

'O ancient Briton, I am pouring out this redness to give life to you. Rise up, O ancient Briton, all this is for you. Rise up and warm yourself. Rise up, O ancient Briton, and quench your ancient thirst.'

I remember that 'quench your ancient thirst', because that was the first time I ever felt the sensation of my hair going freezingly cold, like a cap of solid ice. And I was suddenly afraid. I could see the ancient Briton, deep in the earth, with his corpse teeth bared. Probably his eyes had just flown open. I just knew he would come – and we wouldn't know what to do about it. What could my brother do, when that thing started walking towards us?

My brother was already backing towards me, as if he'd seen something down there in the pit where the stone lay. As he came, he was still trickling wine out onto the tough, leathery grass of the wood. Then he set the bottle down, half-leaning, still with some wine in it, halfway between me and the fire, and joined me. The fire had recovered, the blackberry wine seemed to have helped it.

Perhaps he did other things that I hadn't noticed. We watched the flames and the huge caves of blackness between the tree trunks. Little sparks went writhing up in the reddened smoke. I stared hard, to see a shape beyond them. I kept an eye on the bottle.

I expected something. Maybe a dark lump like an animal would heave itself up out of the hole. Or maybe a person would somehow be there, standing beside the grave, looking towards us.

Or maybe we wouldn't see anything, but the bottle would suddenly rise up in the air and tilt, as an invisible mouth drank at it. Then a shape would grow solid between us and the fire, with the bottle in its hand.

But the worst thought was, if something did come what would we do?

We crouched there, watching the fire till the flames died.

I asked in a whisper if he thought we should go back to the tent, but he hissed so sharp and tense I felt the hair prickle all over my body. He was staring towards the glow of the fire's embers. I tried to see what he was looking at.

'I thought I saw something,' he whispered.

I began to hear sounds in the wood, rustling and tickings. I felt sleepy. Surely the fire had gone out now. He got up at last and walked over to it. I followed him, to stay close. He picked up the bottle, and poured the last drops onto the fire's remains. He turned the altar over with his foot. Nothing had happened.

My little ivory fox came the following summer. This time we were camping in the valley known as Crimsworth Dene.

Our father and mother had both been born in Hebden Bridge. Their paradise had been the deep, cliffy, dead-end gorge of Hardcastle Crags, which cuts back north-west into the moors from Hebden Bridge, full of trees, with a rocky river. The big old mill building still standing there, well up the gorge, was used as a dance hall in those days, where all the boys and girls of Hebden Bridge did their courting. Nowadays, this place is a famous beauty spot. More than once, people from Hebden Bridge, on holiday in Blackpool or Morecambe, have purchased a bus ticket for a day's mystery tour to a beauty spot, and have been brought back to Hardcastle Crags.

Crimsworth Dene is a more secret valley that forks away due north, from the bottom of Hardcastle Crags.

Like all these valleys, Crimsworth Dene is steep-sided, deep, with woods overhanging stone-walled falling-away fields. And above the woods, more stone-walled fields, climbing to a farm or two. And above the farms the moors – the empty prairies of heather that roll away north into Scotland. And in the very bottom of the valley, the dark, deep cleft, thick with beech, oak, sycamore, plunging to an invisible stream.

On the west slope, an old stony packhorse road clambers north between drystone walls, under the hanging woods and above the lower fields, finally up and out across the moor towards Haworth. About a mile up that road, on the left, over the roadway, is a little level clearing.

Perhaps it was once a quarry, for the stone of the local walls. Here, when they were boys, before the First World War, my mother's brothers used to camp. They called Crimsworth Dene 'the happy valley'. The strangest thing that ever happened to me happened there.

One week, my brother decided to camp there. Though it was right in the heart of the territory that belonged, as I felt, to our mother and father, it was a little outside ours. But our uncles knew the farmers, and they had given my brother permission to shoot rabbits and magpies and such like. Now and again he did roam this far with his rifle, but only rarely and briefly. For me, though I had always known Hardcastle Crags, it was the first time I had ever entered Crimsworth Dene. I was still quite young, only seven.

As we pitched our tent on the Friday evening, on that little clearing, under the trees, I knew this was the most magical place I had ever been in. The air was very still, and the sky clear after a warm day. All down the valley, over the great spilling mounds of foxgloves, grey columns of midges hung in the stillness, like vertical smoke above camp-fires. I brought water up from the stream in our rope-handled canvas bucket, and collected dead sticks for firewood, while he sorted our bedding, the pans and cutlery, and made a fireplace with stones. All the while a bird sang on the very topmost twig of a tree over the clearing. I had never heard a bird like it, nor have I since.

It was a thrush, I expect. But every note echoed through the whole valley. I felt I had to talk in whispers. Even so, I thought each word we spoke would be heard in Pecket, away out of sight round the hill's shoulder, a mile or more away.

My brother got a fire going and warmed up our beans. Camping is mainly about camp-fires, food cooked on camp-fires, and going to sleep in a tent. And getting up in the wet dawn. We planned to get up at dawn, maybe before dawn, when the rabbits would be dopey, bobbing about in the long dewy grass. Our precious, beautiful thing, my brother's gleaming American rifle, lay in the tent, on a blanket.

As it grew dark, I kept hearing a tune in my head and the words of the song. It came to me whenever I looked down over the deep grass of the steep field below us towards that plunge of dark trees. Very clear I heard:

If you go down to the woods today
You're sure of a big surprise

and the strange tune of that song, which sounds like a bear romping through a gloomy forest.

As I lay on my groundsheet, under my blanket at last, looking up at the taut canvas of our bell-tent, and listening to the stars, and the huge, silent breathing of the valley, I felt happier than I had ever been. And wider awake than I had ever been. Even so, I went straight off to sleep.

I woke in the dark, thinking it must be time to get up. I lay listening for night creatures. After a long time I began to hear cockcrows, then the tent walls began to pale. My brother woke and, without breakfast, we were off.

Dark tracks of rabbits were everywhere in the white of the heavy dew. I looked at the tracks quite close around our tent. Why hadn't I heard whatever made them? What had made them? Rabbits, or something else?

Usually, one rabbit was all we could expect to shoot. But because this was new hunting ground, and because the place seemed so magically wild, secret and undisturbed, I was hoping for a record bag. We saw hardly a rabbit. Only the odd white tail far off, just glimpsed then gone. The sun rose. The dew glittered and dried. We tramped all over the hillside, up as far as the moor. We skulked along the edges of woods, peering over walls. We had to inspect every tiny thing. It might be a snipe. Or the lifted head of a grouse strayed down off the high ground. But my brother did not fire one shot. For the last part of the morning we stretched out in the heather and he sunbathed.

But then, coming back to our camp for breakfast at midday, we found something curious. The wall along the top of the wood, directly above our camp, had a tumbledown gap. As we came down through that gap, my brother pointed.

Under the wall, on the wood side, a big flat stone like a flagstone, big as a gravestone, leaned outwards, on end. It was supported, I saw, by a man-made contraption of slender sticks. Tucked in behind the sticks, under the leaning slab, lay a dead woodpigeon, its breast torn, showing the dark meat.

'Gamekeeper's deadfall,' said my brother.

It was the first deadfall I had seen set. I had read about them, made of massive tree trunks, used by trappers in the Canadian forests for bears, wolves, wolverines. My brother explained how it worked. How one light touch on the tripstick would collapse the support and bring the great stone slam down flat – on top of whatever was under it.

I went past it warily. I didn't want the jolt of my tread to bring it down.

'The pigeon is fresh,' said my brother. 'He must have baited it yesterday. Or maybe this morning. For a fox, probably.'

We hadn't seen the gamekeeper, who looked after Lord Savile's grouse up on the moor. He only became a danger if you'd shot some of his grouse and this time we hadn't. Still, we'd kept a sharp lookout for him.

A gamekeeper usually sees you first. And the moment he sees you, he becomes invisible – till he's right on top of you.

In the afternoon, we went back up onto the heather. My brother was mad about sunbathing. He rubbed himself with olive oil and lay there frying. I lay for a while. But I wasn't mad about the sun. I left that to him. Eventually, I found a trickle of water that overflowed an old drinking trough and spent the afternoon making dams and channels.

Rabbits usually come out again about four o'clock. But still we had no luck. Somehow, in spite of all the tracks in the dew, and in spite of the silent, lonely emptiness of the valley, rabbits seemed to know better than to show themselves in the day. We ended up drinking tea at a farmhouse, where the farmer said his old mother, who made the tea then sat watching us from a rocking chair in the corner, was some remote cousin of our grandmother. After that, he wanted us to shoot a particular rat. This rat was stealing eggs, according to him. Its front doorway was a crevice under the threshold of an old stable. Every evening he saw it. But it was far too smart to be trapped. He gave us two addled eggs that we propped up, very visible, three yards in front of its hole. Then we climbed to a hayloft, and lay looking down at both eggs and rat-hole, through the open loft door.

We lay there unmoving, on the warm boards, with our eyes on that hole, till the light began to fail. Maybe the rat was watching us from inside his hole. He never appeared. I became impatient, thinking of the rabbits we were missing. They were probably out all over the place. I wanted to take home at least one.

Finally, my brother gave in and we went back down over the fields from the high farm, to our camp. We saw rabbits, but it was too dark now to see the sights of the rifle. Anyway, I found I was more interested in getting to the gap in the wall. I couldn't wait to see the trap. I imagined a great red fox in it, squashed flat. Or maybe a stoat. A stoat would easily trip those frail, balanced sticks. Or maybe even a crow. A stoat might leap clear.

But it yawned there just as we'd left it, and the woodpigeon lay untouched.

My idea of the valley was changing. I had thought of it teeming with stoats, weasels, foxes – as well as rabbits. But here, as everywhere else, perhaps the gamekeepers and the poultry farmers were in control. Even crows. I hadn't seen a crow. I hadn't seen a magpie. A magpie would have found that woodpigeon anywhere in the valley.

But the gamekeeper had set the trap, so there must be something. Maybe, as my brother said, there was a fox. A lone fox, a notorious, solitary bandit, with his hide-out in this wood, near our camp. Among rocks, maybe, where he couldn't be dug out. And maybe tomorrow morning he'd be there, flat under the fallen slab. Or she. It might be a vixen.

The evening was as still as the night before. As we fried eggs and bacon, and our pork and beans to go with them, the magical spell came over me again. The thought of a fox very near, deep in his den, maybe smelling our bacon, made everything more mysterious. I kept looking down through the dusk into the crevasse of dark trees below, to give myself the eerie feeling of that tune again, and the strange words:

> If you go down to the woods today
> You're sure of a big surprise . . .

It never failed. As the valley grew darker, the feeling, with its bear coming up through the forest, grew even stronger. Whenever I looked down there, and thought of that tune, I found I could make myself shiver and freeze. I could do it over and over, looking away and then looking back down there, and hearing the tune – each time I would shiver and freeze afresh. Like touching myself with an electric spark. I kept testing myself to see if it would go on happening. And every time it happened.

The fox would be smelling our bacon all right, and our coffee. We always brewed coffee in the dusk. That was the part I liked best of all, sitting there, gazing into the fire and sipping sweet, scalding coffee, while the thick sticks crumbled to a cave of glow, whitening the hearthstones. Maybe those tracks in the dew last night had been the fox, inspecting us and our fireplace and looking for leftovers.

Again we planned to get up early. Some time tomorrow, Sunday, we would have to set off back home. My brother wanted to bag something as badly as I did. He was regretting wasting time on the rat.

That night I tried to stay awake, so I could have every minute of lying there under my blanket, listening. Each tiny sound had to be something. I could hear the stream, down in the bottom. Why hadn't I heard that the night before? Would I hear a fox if he came right up to the tent wall, and sniffed at me through the canvas?

At some point I drifted off to sleep because when I woke I thought it was dawn. Then I realized, the pale light coming through the canvas was moonlight. I was absolutely alert, and tense. Something had wakened me. I lay there, hardly daring to breathe. Then I heard a whisper, a low hiss of a whisper, outside the tent. It was calling my name.

Somebody was out there. My brother was breathing gently beside me, fast asleep. I simply listened. I don't know what I thought. I felt no fear, but still I was amazed to feel the tears trickling slowly down over my ears, as I lay staring upwards.

The whisper came again, my name. It seemed to be coming from about where the fire was.

Very carefully, partly not to waken my brother, partly not to let the voice know I was listening, I sat up, leaned forward, and tried to peep through the laced-up door of the tent. By holding the edges of the flaps slightly apart, I could see a tiny dot of red glow still in our fireplace. Everything out there was drenched in a grey, misty light.

Somebody was standing beside the fireplace.

It was a person and yet I got the impression it was somehow not a person. Or it was a very small person. It looked like a small old woman, with a peculiar bonnet on her head and a long shawl. That was my impression. As I stared with all my might, trying to make out something definite, this figure drifted backwards into the shade of the trees. But the whisper came again:

'Come out. Quickly. There's been an accident.'

I immediately knew it must be somebody from the farm. Surely it was the farmer's little old mother. That was how she knew we were here. The farmer had fallen down a well, or down a loft ladder, or a mad, calving cow had gored him and crushed his ribs. Or he'd simply tumbled downstairs going to get his old mother a cup of tea because she couldn't sleep.

Something stopped me waking my brother. What I really wanted was to find out more. Who was this person? What was the accident? Anyway, it was my name that had been called. It must be me that was specially needed. I could come back and tell my brother later. Most of all, I wanted to see who this was.

I had gone to sleep in my clothes, to keep warm and for a quick start. So now I pulled on my boots. I unlaced the tent door at the bottom and crawled out. The grass was cold and soaking under my hands.

'Hurry,' came the whisper from under the trees. 'Hurry, hurry.'

It seems strange, that I felt no fear. I was so sure that it was somebody from the farm, that I thought of no other possibility. Only huge curiosity, and excitement. Also, I felt quite important suddenly.

I went toward the voice, staring into the dark shade. The moon was past full but very hard and white. I wanted to get into the shade quickly, where I wouldn't be so visible.

But now the voice came again, from further up the wood. Yes, the voice was climbing towards the farm.

'Hurry,' it kept saying. 'Hurry up.'

Beneath the trees, the slope was clear and grassy, without brambles or undergrowth. Easy going but steep, with that tough, slippery grass.

As I climbed, the voice went ahead. Very soon, I could see through the top of the wood. The bright night sky was piled with brilliant masses of snowy cloud, beyond the dark tree stems. I glimpsed the black silhouette now and again, the funny bonnet, climbing ahead, bobbing between the trees.

'Are you coming?' came the whisper again. 'This way.'

I saw her shape in the gap of the wall, clear against those snowy clouds. Then she had gone through it. It was now, as I came up towards the gap, sometimes grasping tussocks to help myself upwards, that I saw something else, bouncing and scrabbling under the wall, in a clear patch of moonlight.

At first I thought it was a rabbit, just this moment scared into a snare by our approach, now leaping and flinging itself to be free, but tethered by the pegged snare. It was the size of a rabbit. Then I smelt the rich, powerful smell.

With a shock, I remembered. I had come right up to the deadfall.

The great slab of stone had fallen. Beside it sat a well-grown fox cub, staring up at me, panting. As I took this in, the cub suddenly started again, tugging and bouncing, jerking and scrabbling, without a sound, till again it crouched there, staring up at me, its mouth wide open, its tongue dangling, panting.

I could see now that it was trapped by one hind leg and its tail. They were pinned to the ground under the corner of the big slab.

The smell was overpowering, thick, choking, almost liquid, as if concentrated liquid scent had been poured over me, saturating my clothes and

hands. I knew the smell of fox – the overpowering smell of frightened fox.

Then I looked up and saw the figure out there in the field, only five yards away, watching me. More than ever I could see it was a little old woman, with her very thin legs and her funny bonnet and shawl. She did not seem to be wanting me to go to the farm. She had brought me to this fox cub. She was probably some eccentric old lady who never slept, or slept only by day and spent the night roaming the hillsides, talking to owls and befriending foxes. She would have seen our camp. Probably some of those tracks had been hers, brushed through the dew around our tent. Now she had found the trapped cub, and not being strong enough to lift the slab, she had come to us. She wanted me to lift the slab and free the cub. She had not called my brother because she thought he might kill it. She must have watched us, and heard him speak my name.

My first thought was to catch the cub and keep it alive. But how could I hold it and at the same time lift the slab? It was a desperate, ferocious little thing. I could have wrapped it in my jersey, knotting the arms round it. But I didn't think of that. As I put my fingers under the other corner of the slab, the cub snapped its teeth at me and hissed like a cat, then struggled again, jerking to free itself.

With all my strength I was just able to budge the slab a fraction. But it was enough. As the slab shifted, the cub scrabbled and was gone – off down the wood like a rocket.

I looked up at the old lady, and this was my next surprise. The bare, close-cropped, moonlit field was empty. I walked out to where she had been. The whole wide field, under the great bare sky of moonlight, all made much brighter by that great bulging heap of snowy, silvery clouds, was empty. Not even a sheep. Absolutely nothing.

She couldn't have run away. I had looked down for only a few seconds. She had simply gone. I could see every blade of grass where she had stood. The field wall. The trees of the wood. The hilltops above and beyond.

I came back to the deadfall. Now I saw that it lay at a slight tilt. There was something beneath it. Another cub, maybe. I tried again to lift it. But I still could not budge it more than that quarter inch, and only for a second. I could not possibly lift it.

It was as I came back down to our campsite that I saw somebody standing outside the tent, in the moonlight. I stopped, hidden under the trees. With a sudden terrible thought, I remembered the ancient Briton. And now, for the first time, I was really frightened.

But then I heard my name called in a familiar low voice. It was my brother. He had come out of the tent. And now he had heard me.

'Where have you been?'

I told him what had happened. All he said was, 'We'll have a look in the morning. Come and get back to sleep.'

But I lay awake. The tent darkened and became pitch black. Either the moon had gone down or that cloud had come up and covered it. Then I heard the prickling sound of light rain on the canvas.

The rain grew heavier, and soon it was filling the whole world, like a steady tearing of canvas inside my head. A drop hit my face.

Slowly the canvas paled. I heard cocks crowing in the high farms and dozed off. Next thing I smelt bacon. The rain had stopped. It was day.

'Come on, let's eat everything,' called my brother.

I wanted to see the deadfall, but he would not be hurried. We scoured our pans and dishes with grit and water and bundled them into their bag. He began to take down the wet tent. In a few minutes everything was inside a bulging kitbag. The rain had come back by now, but more of a drizzle. It looked to be setting in for the day. The shooting trip was over, I could see.

But now he took his rifle from under the tree where he'd leaned it in the dry with the bag over its muzzle, and started off up the wood.

The deadfall lay as I had left it. He handed the rifle to me, put his fingers under the slab and heaved it back against the wall.

There, at our feet lay a big red fox, quite dead, the woodpigeon still in its mouth.

He pulled it clear and inspected it. The body was stiff. He picked it up by one hind leg. A foreleg stuck out at an angle. Its head was twisted to one side, keeping its grip on the dead bird. Only the tail plumed over, like a fern. I had expected to see whatever was under there flattened like a rat on the road. It did look slightly flattened, its fur was flattened.

Still carrying the dead animal by the one hind leg, my brother took the rifle from me and started off down the wood. But then he turned back, handed me the rifle again, and pulled the deadfall slab over. It dropped with a shocking thud into its position. I felt the earth bounce.

'This fox escaped,' he said.

Down at our campsite, he brought out our little axe. I asked him what we were going to do with the fox. Wasn't it the gamekeeper's? I remember his answer:

'This fox belongs to itself.'

Then he began to dig a hole with the axe in the middle of the patch of grass flattened by our tent. He cut out the turf and set it aside, then hacked downwards, scooping the loosened soil out with his hands, till he began to hit stones. The hole was about two feet deep. He jabbed about down there with a sharpened stick, dislodging stones, and shaping the bottom of the hole. I crouched beside the work, watching the hole and looking at the fox. I had never examined a fox. It was so astonishing to see it there, so real, so near. When I lifted its eyelid, the eye looked at me, very bright and alive. I closed it gently, and stroked it quite shut. Its face was slightly squashed-looking, but with no visible damage, no blood. And so peculiar, with the woodpigeon gripped in its mouth.

My brother picked it up again.

'Do you want its tail?' he asked me. I shook my head.

He fitted it neatly into the bottom of the hole, and arranged it, bending the stiff, jutting foreleg to look more comfortable. We tucked the little stones around it, and covered it with the gritty black soil. Then the turfs. He took out some of the soil and threw it away, to let the turfs lie flat. I helped him push loose soil out of sight down between the sliced turfs. As I was doing this, I felt a knobbly pebble and saw under my fingers what looked like one of those white quartz pebbles you find embedded in the black boulders on the moor. But then I realized it was not a pebble.

I stood up to examine it. I could not believe what I had in my hand. It was this little ivory fox. I was so startled that I simply gripped it. Maybe I thought my brother might take it off me.

'What's wrong?' he asked, looking up. He never missed anything. But I managed to shift my inspection to the back of my fingers. I got my find into my pocket and bent again to the grave. He was combing the grass of the turfs with his fingers, drawing it over the edges, to make it look like unbroken sod again.

When he'd finished, you couldn't really tell it was there, even from quite close. Everything looked like the scuffed and trampled patch where a tent has been. As I stood there, I could feel him watching me. 'Are you all right?' he asked.

We had to walk down into Hebden Bridge, in the drizzle, to catch a bus home. He carried the kit bag, I carried the rifle. He had not fired one shot.

It was while we were waiting at the bus stop that he asked me who I thought the old woman was last night. Well, I said, it must have been just some old woman.

'But you said she vanished.'

'She did. One second she was there, and the next she wasn't.'

'Do you think,' he said, 'it might have been the dead fox's ghost?'

So it was there, standing at the bus stop in Hebden Bridge, that I first had to wonder whether I had seen a ghost. I didn't know what to think about it. But two or three times since then I have seen what seemed to be a ghost, and I know that as soon as the moment's past – you don't know what to think about it. I didn't know what to think about the little ivory fox either – the fox in my pocket. Who could have dropped it where I found it? One of our uncles long ago? Obviously, when a thing's dropped like that it doesn't vanish into the never never. It has to stay right there. So this fox could have been there long before our uncles. Long, long, long before. Like the stones. What made me feel slightly giddy was the way I'd found it while we were actually burying that fox. I did not know what to make of any of it. I could not see any way past it. When I thought about it, I felt a ring tightening round my head.

But there was the ivory fox in my pocket, so smooth and perfect. And after all these years, here it is, just as I found it. And I still do not know what to make of it. Or of that old lady either. If it was an old lady.

Later that year we moved away to another part of Yorkshire. I did not walk up Crimsworth Dene again, to look at the fox's grave, for many, many years.

HURRY PLEASE

BERLIE DOHERTY

Like the narrator of this story, I had always wanted to visit this man's cottage in Dorset. I went first to the churchyard, where his heart is buried, and then followed the woodland path to his home. It is strikingly like my own. When I read the legend on the bedroom wall describing his birth I was deeply moved. I returned next day to read it again, and have been haunted by it ever since.

You see, this story is almost true . . .

June, and a perfect day for this visit, which I had promised myself for many years. I had a childish sense of excitement as I drove towards his cottage, through the lovely countryside of Dorset. My route took me past the church that I'd heard so much about, and on a whim I decided to stop there on my way. The day was blue and bright and welcoming as I parked my car just outside the church. Away on either side of me rolled farmed fields. House martins stitched their route above the churchyard, crisscrossing the sky with their familiar twitching flight, glancing against the walls of the church and away again as if they could never for a moment take rest there. And there were the family graves, all in a line.

It was just as I was looking at them, reading the inscriptions and pondering on the fact that so many of the males of the family bore his name, that I heard a burst of fine, lively music coming from the church. I went to the door and could hear clearly the sound of a violin and a cello, and the sweet, rough singing of country voices. I opened the door slowly, not wanting to intrude on a service but eager to hear the music more clearly. The sounds stopped at once. I pushed open the door fully and went in. There was no one there. Yet there was an echo of the music that lingered still, as though the singers and musicians had only paused, and were waiting for me to leave. I crept round the listening silence of the church and went out again, glad of the warm embrace of sunlight. I closed the door behind me and waited, half-expecting the music to start up, but there was nothing. Yet I was certain I had heard it earlier.

I wanted to take the time, even then, to stroll around the churchyard and look again at the family graves, but something was tugging me away from them. The music had certainly disturbed me, but there was more than that. I had the nagging feeling that something important had been left undone. I couldn't relax there. For a moment, as I stood hesitating in the church porch, it seemed to me that the far horizon was breaking up. Instead of the fields of neat farmland that I had seen before, stretching away into the distance, there seemed to be a vast, dull wilderness. I could hear his words describing it – heathy, furzy, briary. Yet as soon as I came out of the churchyard I realized I was mistaken. The sun had slipped behind the clouds and dulled the light, that was all.

I returned to my car and set off on the last part of the journey, to the cottage. I parked my car and walked half a mile or so along a woodland path. Even though I had lost the full sun now, I was sticky with heat. Patches of sunlight dappled through the leaves and lit clumps of bluebells and around them flies lumbered, heavy with noise. A strange feeling of urgency hurried me on. Of course, I was anxious to arrive.

And at last, there it was, after so many turns and twistings. I saw first the great beech tree at the back of the cottage. I had seen pictures of it so many times that I could have drawn the cottage from memory, with its long thatched roof arching over the latticed windows, and its three tall chimneys. I hurried round to the front. No, this surely was the wrong place. Here were two buildings, leaning against each other, but separate dwellings, surely. They were very clearly a main house with roses and honeysuckle clinging on to its walls and spilling their perfume, and a sort of lean-to that seemed to have been tacked on to the side, with its own doorway. I stepped back a moment to look at the sign but was reassured that I had indeed come to the right place.

There came then a drumming of hooves on the lane behind me, of a horse and cart being driven with great urgency. It pulled up so close to me that I was knocked into the hedge. A man in a long-coated black suit jumped down from the cart and reached up for a black bag. He hurried past me without acknowledging my surprised greeting, down the path and into the house through the main door. Almost immediately the door of the smaller house opened and a white-haired woman came out. She too was dressed in black, in the long skirts of the last century. She followed the man quickly into the main house.

I stood at the gate, confused and curious. Perhaps it was some sort of play, specially devised for the visitors. In that case I had arrived just in time. I heard someone coming up behind me.

'Would you hurry, please,' a woman's voice said. I turned, and saw no one. 'Hurry.' I looked the other way, and distinctly felt a movement of air as if someone was brushing past me. I stepped back, then heard the click of the gate behind me. A faint sweat of fear came over me, yet still there was that nagging sense of urgency and purpose. I opened the gate and closed it, tried it again, and it gave exactly that sound I had heard. Someone had come through it. Very gently, I closed it again, and turned to the house. There, in front of me, was the cottage I had always expected; a long single building with a path winding its way through a garden of lupins and lavender to the one front door. There was no sign now of the cart and horse, of the hurrying people. I had imagined everything.

I had come there intending to linger first in the garden and then to wander around his cottage, taking my time to explore the rooms. Now all I wanted was to turn away and go back through the woods and drive home. Perhaps I would return another time, maybe with a friend. Yet I had travelled so far to be here. I had even made an appointment to come. It didn't matter. I could come another time, I told myself. I paused with my hand on the gate. The woman's voice I had just heard echoed in my head. 'Would you hurry, please.' I had heard it, and the click of the gate, the scuff of her boots on the path. I had not seen that person, but she had seen me. I had not imagined it. I had to go in.

I was greeted at the door, as if I had been expected, and was invited to walk straight into the parlour to the left of the porch.

'You've had a lot of visitors this morning,' I said lightly.

'Not at all. You're the first to come today,' I was told.

'And the play?' I felt foolish saying it. 'Has it started?'

'What play do you mean?' The warden shook his head and smiled.

I went through to the parlour feeling more than a little anxious. Yet the room was peaceful and calm. It smelled of polish, and had the quiet and ordered appearance that rooms acquire when they have not been lived in for a great deal of time. It was a show room. I glanced casually round, recognizing the room from descriptions I had read, the floor 'footworn and hollowed and thin', the one long beam bisecting the low ceiling, and the deep inglenook fireplace, long empty of wood ash. I crossed over to the second of the two windows. I could almost hear his voice then, chanting in my head:

'Here was the former door, where the dead feet walked in.'

I tried to shake the words away. He had come from a family of builders – all kinds of changes would have been made to the house. At the far end of the room was a thin wooden door leading, as I knew, to his father's office, and through there to the stairs. I was unwilling to go that way yet. I felt I wanted to be out in the sunlight. I was cold. I touched the glass of the window where the flowers pressed against it and there it came again, as clear as it had been in the garden outside, the commotion of hurrying feet, the scuff of boots on stone. I felt the cool sensation of someone brushing past me, and heard again the words, 'Would you hurry, please,' and knew that they were being spoken to me. But the room was empty, the only sound was the birdsong in the garden outside. I called out, 'Who's there?' The house was in silence. And yet now, at the same time, it was full of sound and movement, of panic even. I ran through to the porch, shouting, 'Didn't you see someone then, a woman? Did you let her in?' The porch was deserted.

I was just at the point of running through into the garden when I heard the sound of a woman crying out in pain from one of the upstairs rooms.

The sound echoed round the house, rolling from room to room. Frightened though I was, it was my instinct to turn back to the porch and to run right through the parlour and up the stairs. I went straight into the main bedroom of the house. This, I was sure, was where the cry came from. There was not a soul to be seen there. I was about to go through to the further room when I heard a sharp intake of breath, a gasp here, a sigh from the other side – all around me, it seemed, unseen people were breathing. Then the sounds quietened down.

I steadied myself, and made myself take the time to look around me. The room was light, having windows at each side, but cool because of the low thatch which kept most of the sunlight out. The floorboards were of fine old chestnut, and most of the room was taken up by a large bed. There was certainly nobody in the room.

As I crossed over to go to the next room the gasping started again. I pressed my hands against my eyes, wishing myself well and sane again, heard footsteps on the stairs, and looked round. I had not been aware before that there was a fire lit in the grate, setting the room moving with the flickering dance of flame and shadow. Surely I would have noticed that, and been grateful for its heat. Someone was pushing past me, breathless, as if they were carrying an awkward burden. I heard the slop of water, and saw then in the firelight's shadows, half in and half out of real light, the old white-haired woman setting down a large and steaming bowl by the bed.

Now other shapes came dimly into view. They were fragmented and unfocused, shapes and shadows first, and then they began to take form and a degree of colour. There were several people in the room. A young man was over by one of the windows, substantially blocking out the light. He had his back to the room. The older man who had arrived in the coach was stooping over the bed. He was in his shirt sleeves, and his long coat was hanging by a nail on the back of the door. By his pose I could imagine that he was a doctor. In the bed was a young woman. She was pale, lying back as if she was exhausted. A mob-capped nurse on the other side of the bed leaned across and wiped her face with a cloth. The young woman gave another gasp of pain, and I turned away towards the other window, to the reassurance of sunlight cutting out a small gold square on the floorboards. Musical instruments were leaning against the wall, a violin and a cello, put down as if carelessly, in a moment of anxiety. I wanted to touch them, to make sure for myself that they were real. Without realizing it I was walking on tiptoe. I hardly dared to breathe.

As I moved, I put my hand out carefully to touch the bed, to touch the figures there, to touch the instruments. There was nothing. Slowly I paced the circumference of the room, frightened almost of displacing the air with my movement. Where the figures had been there was nothing. I felt an overwhelming sense of dread and loss, and into that sensation came the voice which I had no doubt belonged to the doctor,

'It's a boy,' he said quietly. 'But I'm afraid, Jemima, he is dead.'

He lifted up the pale, still body of a baby and, rolling it in a sheet, put it aside on a chair and bent to attend to the woman again. The man at the window, surely the husband, gave a gasp of dismay and came to the bed. It was evident to me that it was too painful for him to look at the baby. He sat down on the edge of the bed and took the young woman's hands in his own, murmuring out soft words of comfort to her. The older woman, his mother maybe, sighed and crossed herself. The doctor poured water from the jug at the wash-stand and soaped his hands. He was distressed. He had done his job as well as he could. 'I'll leave you to the monthly nurse and to your family,' he said. 'I have more work to do in the village.'

Those moments seemed to last for ever. There was nothing to be done, nothing anyone could do, it seemed. The family quietened into a sad, exhausted resignation. Yet now, over their silence I could hear the sound of other voices, rising and falling in echo, clamouring for attention. They seemed to be coming from every corner of the room, from the fields outside, from the air itself – I felt I could drown in the welter of sounds, the voices of men and women and children, soldiers and farmers and country girls, marching and dancing and calling out, their words jostling like the insistent buzzing of summer insects in a garden. Every now and again I caught something familiar in the words they were saying, as if I had heard them spoken before, as if they were shouting to me out of my memory. I was washed in their sea of sadness and panic. And clearly through all the sounds came that first voice again, at my side this time, a woman's voice speaking to me. 'Would you hurry, please.'

34

None of the family in the room had looked at the dead baby on the chair. I crouched down to it, anxious to catch a glimpse of what might have been. I knew exactly who it was. I was sure then that I saw just the tiniest movement of his fingers. It was as if a butterfly had moved tiny wings. Surely he was alive.

There it came again. It was the slightest flexing of a finger. I put my cheek to his lips, and felt the smallest kiss of air. He was alive.

'He's not dead!' I shouted. 'Listen to me. He's not dead!'

But there was no way of making them hear me. The doctor rolled down his sleeves, the nurse held out his coat for him. Then the old mother stooped to pick up the bowl and carry it away. The husband drew close the curtains so his young wife could sleep.

'He's not dead!' I shouted into their faces, but there was nothing I could do to make them listen to me. I tried to lift up the child but my hands slipped through empty air. And still the voices clamoured round me, begging for attention.

'He's not dead!' I shouted again. Frantic now, I looked round for some way of attracting the attention of the figures in the room. I felt in my pockets and found there the book that I had brought, and that I had been reading again the night before. Instinctively I flung it on the floor in front of the nurse, just as she was handing the doctor his bag. As if something had startled her, she looked towards the direction of the sound. There was no book there for her to see. She heard the sound from somewhere in her imagination, I think.

Slowly she put down the bag and reached over to where the baby was bundled up in its shawl. With one hand to her mouth she moved away a corner of the sheet. The baby's first unclenched.

'Dead!' she cried. 'Stop a minute! He's alive enough, sure!'

I leaned back against the wall, faint with exhaustion. The voices drizzled around me, too fragmented now to catch. I saw the doctor and the nurse attending to the child, heard at last his first strong cry, saw him being lifted into the air and put into his young mother's arms.

'Thomas,' her husband said. 'Young Thomas Hardy is born.'

In the way that the shadows of moving shapes are cast by firelight around a room and then extinguished, so the figures in the room dissolved. A great peace descended on the house, and on me. I believe I went into a kind of deep sleep there, standing as I was. Certainly I was startled into wakefulness by the sound of a sudden burst of laughter coming from outside. I looked out of the window, into the dazzle of sun, and saw that the garden was full of people, visitors like myself, taking photographs, crouching to smell the flowers. Soon the house would be invaded by them. Already now I could hear voices in the room below me. I went through the narrow doorway and heard footsteps behind me.

'Just a moment,' a young woman said.

I knew her voice.

I turned, and she came softly towards me, holding out a book. 'I think you dropped this.'

I took it from her. '*Tess of the D'Urbervilles*,' I said. 'I would hate to lose this. Thank you.'

'Not at all,' she said, and turned to go away. 'Thank *you*.'

SILVER GHOST

MICHAEL MORPURGO

There are very few grand houses in North Devon. Those that did exist have long since fallen into disrepair, their estates unable to sustain them.

One or two have survived though, and amongst them a relatively unknown National Trust house – the nearest Trust property to where I live in Iddesleigh. The photograph I saw in a guidebook was of a handsome, but modest house, a little plain perhaps. Anyhow, it was close, so I went over to have a look.

The parkland was rolling and gracious, the driveway imposing, but at first glance I could see no house. Then I discovered there was no house, not any more. All I found was a plaque on a wall telling me the house had been destroyed by fire.

No one knows how or why the fire started. Until now.

At about six o'clock on the evening of 14 November 1969, a young man came into the pub at Nethercott Cross and asked for a beer. He took it away to a corner table by the fire and began to write feverishly in a notebook. When the landlord crouched down beside him to unload an armful of logs, he scarcely looked up, so engrossed was he in his writing. After some time he shut his notebook, sat back in his chair and sipped his drink, gazing into the fire. The pub cat jumped up onto his lap. 'So you recognize me too, do you?' he said, laughingly.

'Should he?' said the landlord from the bar.

'Well, Mr Glanville recognized me, up at Nethercott.'

'Mr Glanville?'

'He said I looked just like one of the portraits up there – "spitting image" he called it – and I did too. He showed me. The one in the Justice Room – it was like looking in a mirror.'

The landlord was puzzled. 'Who are you? Where you from?'

'Nat. Nathaniel Bickford,' replied the young man. 'I'm from Vermont, in the US. I've been looking for my English roots. My folks lived up at Nethercott – way, way back, hundred years or more. What a place! And the things that old Mr Glanville told me. Quite a story.'

'Percy Glanville?' said the landlord. 'Little bent sort of fellow? Silvery hair? Old as the hills?'

'That's the guy,' said Nat.

The landlord stood for a moment, frowning. 'So he's home again then, is he?' he said at last. 'I thought the old boy was still in hospital. Got a dicky heart. Well, I expect I'll be seeing him soon then. He spends half his life in here – not that I'm complaining, mind. But between you and me, he drinks too much. He writes poetry too. Bit of a strange one, if you know what I mean.'

That was the last time they spoke. Nathaniel Bickford, an aspiring poet himself, decided he didn't like the landlord. He stood with his back against the fire and drank down his beer quickly. He wrapped his multi-coloured scarf round his neck, picked up his rucksack and walked out into the darkness.

Later, the landlord would recall every word that had passed between them. He would remember the rainbow-coloured scarf, the young man's American accent, his height – about six foot one, his long, fair hair with a band around it like tennis players wear, and the exact time the young man had left. He told the police: 'I'd say he stayed for about half an hour, no more. So he must have left just after six-thirty.'

At half-past seven that same evening, Gabriel Penberthy, who grazed his sheep on the parkland around Nethercott House, looked out of his bathroom window at home. He noticed that every light up in the house seemed to be on and he thought that was strange, because no one lived there. The place was due to be opened to the public in a week. There was some plumbing work still being done, but he remembered seeing the plumber's van rattling off down the drive at dusk. No one else should have been up there. Gabriel Penberthy pulled aside the net curtain, opened the window and looked out. Then he saw that the lights were not lights at all but flickering flames. The house was ablaze from end to end. He could see smoke now, rising black into the moonlit night and sparks were funneling up from the chimney stacks.

It was Gabriel Penberthy who called the fire brigade. The fire engines came from Holsworthy, Torrington and Hatherleigh. But they were too late and too few. Nothing could be done.

Meanwhile Nathaniel Bickford had at last hitched a ride back into Hatherleigh in a smelly Land Rover with a calf in the back. The driver sniffed and wiped his nose with his sleeve, eyed Nat with suspicion but said nothing all the way there. Back in his bedroom at The George, Nat had a deep and steaming bath, and shivered the cold out of him. Afterwards he lay on his bed and read through the notes he'd made back at the pub at Nethercott Cross. The extraordinary events of the day and the old man's story had set his mind racing. He decided to write it down right away so that he lost none of the detail of it, so that it was fresh in his head. He sat propped up against a pile of pillows, put his diary against his knees and the notebook on the bed beside him and began to write.

November 18th

I have walked today the soil my ancestors walked a hundred years ago. I have sat in the chairs my ancestors sat in a hundred years ago. I have stretched out on their beds. I have rummaged through their cellars. In my rucksack I have a handful of ancestral acorns and I shall plant them back home in Vermont. They'll grow roots in Spring Farm soil just as my family did a century ago. Mission accomplished. Roots discovered. But roots wasn't all I discovered today. In the process I came up with something a whole lot more interesting.

This is my second night at The George – very quaint and olde England, thatched roof, oak beams to hit your head on, and genuine cobwebs from the sixteenth century. And beer! Last night I drank a lot of their warm beer, too much. Why do I always drink too much? I managed to struggle out this morning in time for a late breakfast – bacon and eggs and sausages. No maple syrup, no waffles, but breakfast is about the best thing the Brits do when it comes to food. I thumbed a ride through a kind of marshy, dank wasteland and found myself at Nethercott House – the 'family seat' – at about noon. Some guy in a tractor dropped me at the end of the drive, said I had a long walk ahead of me, and that there'd like as not be no one up there in the house to let me in. Gloomy kind of a guy, lugubrious. He turned out to be right. It was a long way up that drive, but the sight of Nethercott House standing proud, looking down over its wonderful rolling parkland, beckoned me on.

Some might think it a plain sort of a house, brick-built, symmetrical, a bit severe perhaps. But it suits the place. It fits in the landscape just like it grew there. Not large enough to dominate, not small enough to be ignored, it simply belongs. I had to keep reminding myself as I walked up the drive. This is really it! This is where the Bickfords come from. This is my place. And the lugubrious guy on the tractor was proved right again. Except for an old pick-up truck parked at the side of the house there was no one about.

The house was bathed in cold autumn sunlight and there was a stillness over the place that made it all seem unreal. Only the sheep moved, scattering when I came near and looking at me with accusing eyes, wishing me away. The flock drifted into the valley, bleating balefully at me. I bleated right back and laughed aloud at them. That was when I happened to glance up at the house. I saw a face in an attic window, hands flat on the windowpane either side of it, a face that fixed me with a look so hostile that I hesitated about venturing any nearer. Hell no, I thought, I've come all this way across the Atlantic to see this place. I'm not letting a pair of eyes scare me off. I waved cheerily at the face and it vanished at once. I walked on, steeling myself.

It was some minutes later that I first heard the knocking, metal on metal or wood on metal. I couldn't be sure which. It came not from the house itself, but from the woods behind and beyond. I passed alongside a high stone garden wall, the knocking so regular that I thought it must be mechanical. Through the trees I glimpsed open garage doors; and inside, a large car shrouded in a white sheet. The knocking had stopped, and then out of the hollow silence came a man's voice, and none too friendly.

'Give us a hand here, will you?' The man wasn't just old, he was ancient. He had a mallet in his hand. The gas tank beside him was covered in ivy.

'Beggaring tap's stuck again,' he said. 'You have a go.'

The tap moved at the second blow and came free at the next. The gas poured out into the can below, splashing over my feet. I stepped back quickly and almost tripped. The old man had me by the elbow and steadied me. 'We'll wipe it off inside,' he said and turned off the tap. When he turned around he was beaming at me. He took off his flat cap and held out a shaky hand. 'I'm Percy Glanville,' he said. 'I live here. This is my place.' The old man's hand was cold in mine. His face was shrunken and shrivelled with age. There was a grey pallor in his cheeks, and his eyes were bloodshot, as if he had not slept for a year. His coat – a khaki military coat – had no buttons and was tied around his waist with string. The only thing clean about him was his silver hair.

'Is it your car?' I asked him. I was curious to know what was under the covers.

'Oh yes. She's mine.' His eyes twinkled with excitement. 'You want to see her?'

'She looks like a ghost under that sheet,' I said.

'Funny you should say that,' he chuckled, and he took hold of the sheet. 'Close your eyes. Go on . . . now you can open them.' The car shimmered silver in the sunlight. It shone so brightly that my eyes hurt and I had to turn away.

'Well?' The old man was at my shoulder.

'It's magnificent,' I said, running my hand along her cold bonnet. 'Old Rolls-Royce, isn't it?'

'1921 Rolls-Royce. Silver Ghost. Park Ward body. We had her from new. She's only done 21,000 miles in forty-eight years, and I drove every one of them myself. That's the best car in the world you're looking at, and she's mine. Worth a fortune too, but I'd never sell her. You want to see inside her?' He never waited for a reply. He showed me over the engine, which was as highly polished as the rest. He told me how he had only recently ground down the pistons. Every detail of the car was a marvel to him, from the red badge on the radiator, to the walnut dash, to the matching suitcases in the carpeted boot. I never knew that anyone could love a car so much.

'She needs petrol,' he said, unscrewing the cap. 'Be a good lad and pour it for me, will you?' It was a moment or two before I remembered that 'petrol' was gas. I used a funnel, but the can was awkward and the angle wrong, so that by the time I had finished, my trousers were spattered with gas.

'We'll put her to bed and then we'll have a cup of tea, shall we?' said the old man. And between us we draped the Silver Ghost in her sheet, closed the garage doors and left her there in the dark. He lived next to the garage. It was a dingy place, and there was an all-pervading stench of drink and cats. The cats, perhaps a dozen of them, came yowling round us. The room was strewn with scraps of paper, written on and discarded; and everywhere there were books, and bottles – empty whisky bottles.

He talked at me from the kitchen, suddenly full of questions. Who was I? What was I doing here? But I had the feeling either that he wasn't interested in my answers or that he knew the answers already – how, I could not imagine.

It unnerved me, but I told him just the same, about how the family had left Nethercott a hundred years before to go sheep farming in Vermont, how we don't keep sheep anymore, just maple trees for syrup and Jersey cows for milk and how I'd always wanted to come back and find my English roots. I sat smothered in cats, sipping hot, sweet tea, and in the intermittent silences thumbing through a much-used copy of Longfellow's poems that I'd found on the table in front of me. As he sat down in the chair opposite me, I told him about the face I'd seen in the attic window. He didn't seem to hear. So I asked again, louder. Still no answer. He stirred his tea slowly. I tried another question. 'Who does Nethercott belong to now?' I asked.

When he looked up at me his eyes had turned suddenly cold and hard. 'You ask too many questions,' he said, an edge to his voice. 'But if you must know, the house belongs to me. Everything here belongs to me, the car, the house, everything. I worked for it, didn't I? I'm not like your kind. I was born with nothing, nothing but a name. No roots to go looking for. No ancestors. My people were always the mounds in the graveyards. No stones to mark where we are. When we're alive no one cares. When we're gone no one cares.' He sat back in his chair, nursing his mug of tea in his lap. 'I've got nothing to hide, nothing to be ashamed of. I'm over ninety. I was in the war, the Great War – 1914-18. Bengie was a young Lieutenant, eighteen, hardly shaving. If you're a Bickford, then he'd be a cousin of yours, I suppose. I was his batman, servant if you like. Same age as he was. Like brothers we were, looked out for each other. Somehow we lived through it all and he brought me back here to be his farm manager and to look after him. He bought the Silver Ghost new in 1921. If I die, he says, the car's yours. He was always talking about dying. He had the gas in the war – weak lungs. He was never really well after that. Thirty years near enough, we lived here, happy as you like. Bit of a poet he was, but his eyes weren't too good, so I'd read to him and that way I became a bit of a poet myself – still am. We did everything together, him and me. We went fishing, hunting, played cards. Sometimes we'd just sit and talk for hours on end. He always told me, "I've got no one else to leave the place to, Percy, so I'm leaving it all to you." And I believed him. I believed him!'

He shook his head and wiped his watery eyes. Then he went on. 'If he ever wanted to go anywhere, and it wasn't often, I'd drive him. He loved that car as much as I do. We looked after her together. No mechanics, just him and me. Then one day I goes to fetch him from the station in the car and he's got this . . . woman with him. Helen May Lasky. He's met her at the races and he's gone and married her. He never asks me, mind you, just goes ahead and does it. And would I mind going and living in the stables? Would I mind! Oh, they made it nice enough for me – inside bathroom, electrics, and I had the Silver Ghost to talk to next door.' As he talked now, the tears were running down his cheeks into the corners of his mouth. 'I wouldn't have minded, but she was always so high and mighty with me. I never hated anyone as much, not even the Germans I fought in the trenches, no one. She felt just the same about me too, and she didn't trouble to hide it either. She said I wasn't to call him Bengie, like I always had. I had to call him "Sir", and I had to call her "Madam". I could see Bengie hated it, but he would never argue with her, never. He was sick with love for her, bewitched he was. Can't think why. She never looked after him like she should have. She was always letting him catch chills. I warned her. I warned her. I told her times he wasn't to get cold and wet else he'd have his chest trouble again. She wouldn't listen. She knew best. So she goes fishing with him, early in the season, March it was and driving wind and rain. He comes back looking like death. He knew it was the finish of him. He told me I had to promise to look after her, so what else could I do? He was dead by the summer, twenty years ago last June. I sprinkled his ashes on the croquet lawn, and she watches from the window because it's raining. We liked croquet, Bengie and me. Nothing better on a summer's evening. But Bengie lied to me. He left everything to her. Oh, I had my cottage for my lifetime, but everything else – the car, the house, everything he'd promised me, he left to her. And that's not the half of it. She calls me in the day after I'd spread his ashes. She wants to buy me off. She'll pay me a thousand pounds if I leave the cottage tomorrow. I was tempted, I can tell you. But I didn't want to live anywhere else.

And besides, I'd promised Bengie, hadn't I? So I stayed, and it was a good thing for her that I did. She wouldn't listen now any more than when Bengie was alive. She wasted all the money Bengie had left her on breeding horses that ran fast as the wind in her head but slow as carthorses on the racing tracks. The money was running out. The cook had to leave, then the housemaids, then the farm labourers. In the end there was just me – cook, butler, stable lad, chauffeur and shepherd, all in one. And never a kind word, never a smile in all those years. She'd sit in her chair in the Justice Room, talking to herself about her horses. No one came near the place, and that was fine by me. If ever they did, she'd drive them off with a shotgun and I'd help her. Just about the only thing we ever agreed on. We liked the place to ourselves. And then, about three years ago now, I found her sitting there in her chair staring out of the window, but her eyes weren't seeing. I closed them. I scattered her ashes on the croquet lawn where I had scattered Bengie.

'I had hopes after she died, high hopes. After all, I'd done everything for her, everything, hadn't I? She had no family, no friends. And I had a right to it. Didn't I have a right to something? So what does she do? She's got no one to leave it to, so she leaves it to everyone. She goes and leaves it all to the National Trust. All her life she hated people coming onto the place, and she knew I hated it too. She knew it! She did it to spite me. That's why next week, if she has her way, there'll be thousands of people trampling all over my place. And it is my place. Bengie promised me. I don't want them here. I won't have them! I won't allow it! I won't!' And he slapped the arm of his chair, slopping the tea onto his trousers. He sat glaring at me, his lips trembling. I didn't know what to say, so I said the first thing that came into my head.

'About the man I saw?' I asked him, 'the face in the attic window.'

'Just the plumber, I expect,' he said, 'come to put the tank in the attic. He's been finishing off for weeks.' He seemed to be struggling to compose himself. He went on. 'He'll be gone by now. He locks up, but I've got a secret key of my own. I expect you'll be wanting to see over the place, will you?' I thought he'd never ask.

I followed him down through the vegetable garden, a frail figure tottering ahead of me in the gloom, and talking as he went. 'I used to grow the best leeks in all Devon in this garden,' he said. 'And I dug the earliest potatoes too. Beautiful.'

We came at last into a dark courtyard behind the house. 'They don't like me going in,' he said. 'But I go where and when I please. Like I told you, it's my place.' The door opened and a light came on inside. 'You can find your own way round,' he said over his shoulder. 'I can't manage the stairs anymore. I'll wait for you in the Justice Room. That way.' And he stabbed a crooked finger in the direction of a closed door at the end of a dark corridor.

For half an hour maybe, I explored the house. I began in the huge kitchens and went down the stone steps into the vaulted cellars. In the dining-room I sat alone at the end of the long polished table gazing up at the portraits of my ancestors. None of them were smiling, and as I left the room I noticed that their eyes were following me out. I felt I was not at all welcome, that they were glad to see the back of me. The drawing-room was sumptuous and grand – oriental carpets everywhere, veneered wood the colour of honey, landscape pictures on the walls and the most capacious armchairs I ever saw. I sank deep into one of them and stretched out my legs, my heels resting on the brass fenders. I had to imagine the log fire and the wolf hounds at my feet, but it wasn't difficult.

After that I went upstairs and along the dark corridors. I looked in on each and every one of the bedrooms – I must have tried out a dozen beds. I was lying on the four-poster bed in the biggest bedroom, dreaming my grand illusions, when I heard footsteps above me. Someone was moving about up in the attic. I remembered the plumber, and thought no more of it. It was some time before I could find my way back to the hallway where I had begun my tour. I opened the door at the end of the corridor and found the old man standing by the fireplace in a magnificent room with ornate plaster ceilings and chandeliers – by far the biggest and grandest room in the house.

'There you are,' he said. 'I was wondering where you'd got to. The Justice Room they used to call this. But there is no justice, is there, not in this world? There's only revenge. An eye for an eye. Bengie and me, we read poetry in here. We wrote a bit too. We'd play cards at that table over there. He shouldn't have treated me the way he did, he shouldn't have done it.' He leaned heavily on the back of a chair and looked around him. 'And that's where she sat in her chair looking out over the park. That's where I found her the day she died.' He was looking straight at me now, almost into me. 'I've been thinking – the soldier in the picture up there above the fire, he was a Bickford. He looks just like you, the spitting image, I'd say. Come to think of it, you and Bengie, you're just like he was when we came back here after the war. You seen all you want, have you?'

'The plumber's still here,' I said. 'I heard him up in the attic. I thought he'd gone.'

'Finishing off, always finishing off.' The old man turned away. 'I'll show you the croquet lawn if you like. Bengie always beat me at croquet. He cheated and I let him. He cheated at cards too, and I let him. But he cheated me once too often. They both did.'

We went outside and stood in front of the house on the croquet lawn. A mist was shrouding the valley and a white screecher owl flew low and silent over the fields. 'Not many of they owls left,' said Percy Glanville. 'You'd best be going. It's getting dark.'

And so I thanked him and left him standing on the lawn. I jumped the open ditch and walked down across the field towards the road. When I turned to wave, he was gone. I noticed too that the plumber's pick-up truck was gone. The last glint of red sun set fire to the attic window, the same window where I'd seen the face earlier that afternoon. I stopped only to collect a handful of red oak acorns to take home with me, souvenirs, so I wouldn't forget. Not that I'm likely to. My last sight of the house was from the bridge over the stream. It glowered at me through the mist and I was suddenly very relieved my family had decided to move to Vermont when they did. I was glad I hadn't been born there.

Has it been worth it, worth coming all this way just to see an old house? I think so. At least I know now where I come from and maybe, just maybe, that'll help to show me where I'm going – you never know. Then there's that old man and his story. You could write a whole book about that. I won't sleep tonight, that's for sure, thinking about him and that face in the window, and the plumber I heard but I never saw – unless he was the face in the window. I guess I'll never know.

•

I'm suddenly hungry. So I'll have a quick shower and grab a sandwich downstairs and a glass or two of their warm beer. I know I shouldn't, but like Oscar Wilde says: 'I can resist just about everything except temptation,' or something like that.

Then I'll have an early night. London tomorrow, then home. I'll be back in Vermont the day after. Two days Devon to Vermont – that's a whole lot quicker than it was for my ancestors.

A fire engine just went wailing by. A little toy of a thing compared to ours at home. I saw a house burning once back in Woodstock when I was a kid. It was a lovely starlit night, I remember, just like tonight. That fire was the most beautiful sight I ever saw and the most terrible too.

There was only one suspect and his trail was easy enough to follow. The plumber had seen a young man with a rucksack come walking up the drive towards the house. The landlord at the Nethercott Cross pub had served a young American a beer and listened to his tale of how he'd been visiting Nethercott House, searching for his roots. He'd even told him his name. And then at The George, Nathaniel Bickford had signed his name in the visitors' book; and everyone remembered the rainbow scarf. The farmer in the Land Rover who gave him a lift back to Hatherleigh remembered the stench of petrol on the young man. That was why he rang the police when it came on the television about the fire and about how the police were looking for a young American with a rucksack and wearing a rainbow-coloured scarf. Nathaniel Bickford had left so many clues behind him, it was almost as if he wanted to be caught.

The police tracked him down at Exeter St David's station. He was sitting on his rucksack waiting for the London train. Back at the police station, he told them everything just as it happened. He'd recorded it in his diary, he said. He handed it over willingly enough. He'd done nothing wrong. He'd help all he could. All he wanted was to get it over with, he said. He had a plane to catch. The detective read the diary carefully, making notes as he did so. When he'd finished he sucked on his pencil and looked across the table at Nat.

'There's just a few little things wrong with your story,' he said.

'What do you mean "wrong"?' said Nat, unable any longer to hide his impatience.

'This old man you mention, this Mr Glanville. He lived up there all right, in the cottage, like you say. We know that. But he doesn't any longer. He died two days ago in Barnstaple, in hospital. Heart failure. So it's hardly likely you were talking to him yesterday afternoon, is it? And that car, the Silver Ghost? We know about the car too. But it was never there yesterday, any more than Percy Glanville was. It was sold when the old lady died and that was three years ago. Made a fortune in the salerooms up in London. That's where they found the money to do the place up. But it broke his heart, poor old boy. Everyone around knows how much he loved that car. That was when he took to the drink.' Nat could feel his heart pounding. 'You're in deep trouble, young man, and what's worse, you're cocky with it, aren't you? You were so sure you were going to get away with it, you didn't even bother to wash your trousers, did you? You stink of petrol, you know that? What d'you think we are over here, stupid?' He waved the diary in Nat's face. 'And as for this. Fantasy!

Storytime! But unfortunately for you there's a dead giveaway in it, right at the end, the bit about how you think a big fire's the most beautiful thing in the world. You wrote it, son. It's all in here.'

No matter how vociferously Nat insisted and argued, he could feel the incriminating evidence building up against him and around him like a wall. It was a nightmare he longed to wake from, but could not.

The police were convinced by now that they had enough evidence to hold Nathaniel Bickford on suspicion of arson. Then the report came in from the Fire Officer. The police expected it to confirm their suspicions. It did not. It said the fire had definitely not been started by petrol. The evidence was quite clear. It was started by a blow-torch left on in the attic. They had found it there, fused in the heat to the gas cylinder and the water tank. There was no question about it. The plumber must have left his blow-torch on and that was how the fire had begun. Probably an accident. There was certainly no evidence of arson. They had to let him go.

Nathaniel Bickford went home to Vermont the next day. Nearly thirty years later and he's never been back to England. As he always says when he tells the story, 'Once was quite enough.'

And on Spring Farm near Woodstock in Vermont, if you look in amongst the maple trees down by the Sugar House, you'll find a single young oak tree growing straight and strong, the only survivor of the acorns he brought back all those years ago from England. In the autumn its leaves are a flicker of red flame in amongst the glowing gold of the maples. Nathaniel Bickford never passes it without remembering.

THE RISING STONES

JOHN QUINN

I like to fuse past and present. The idea of Coney Island, County Armagh as a place of refuge in the past attracted me and the causeway seemed an ideal 'bridge' between past and present. This story was written at a time of great atrocities in Northern Ireland (Shankill and Greysteele) so it was inevitable that they would find echo here.

Karen pressed her nose against the windowpane of the car. Two raindrops careered down the glass on either side of her nose. They might well have been her tears . . .

Gander was dead. Gander Hughes. Her grandfather. It was Karen's childish attempts to utter his name that had bestowed the name 'Gander' on him. The name stuck, and for most of Karen's fourteen years Owen Hughes had been known, to family and neighbours alike, as 'Gander'. Not that he had minded. Not at all. In fact, he took a particular delight in the name and milked it for all it was worth. Karen could still vividly remember him tickling her as he dandled her on his knee by the open fire and sang:

> Goosey, goosey, gander
> Where shall I wander?
> Upstairs, downstairs
> In my lady's chamber

before the two of them collapsed in hysterical laughter. And she could only have been four when he would seat her on the crossbar of his bicycle and set off for The Coney Bar, despite the protestations of his wife.

'We'll be grand!' he would call out. 'We're only going for a wee drop of sauce for the Gander! Me and the wee goslin'.'

Three hours later they would begin their perilous return home, Gander 'taking the two sides of the road' (as his wife would inevitably accuse him), laughing and singing, his whisky breath deliciously warm on Karen's face . . .

The funeral cortege wound its way slowly down that same road now. Karen leaned her cheek against the cold, damp glass. Uncle Hugh crouched over the steering wheel and spoke in a low monotone to her mother, who rocked her head to and fro as she twisted a handkerchief constantly around her index finger. Karen knew this was a heavy blow for her mother. Grandmother Hughes had died five years previously. Now Gander was gone. Both of them had carried her mother through the heaviest blow of all when Karen's father made the mistake of choosing to walk home on a warm Belfast evening fourteen years previously and had walked straight into a car bomb. Karen had never known her father and so it happened that she had spent fourteen summers with Gander and Bessie Hughes.

A watery sun broke through the morning mist. Karen wiped the glass with the back of her hand. The hazel wood appeared almost magically with the stroke of her hand. Kylenadree . . .

'Kyle-na-dree?' The young girl repeated the word slowly.

'That's it,' Gander whispered, taking her hand in his long, slender fingers. 'Kylenadree – the wizard's wood.'

'What's a wizard, Gander?'

'A wise man, goslin'. A very wise man – with magic powers.' He spoke in hushed reverential tones, as if he expected the wizard to step out from behind a hazel tree. 'They say he knew the answer to all problems. And do you know where he got all his knowledge?'

The girl shook her head in puzzlement. The old man released her hand and bent down to pick a handful of hazelnuts.

'That's what he lived on!' He pressed the nuts into her hand. 'So if you want to grow up to be a wise woman you must eat lots of these!' he chuckled.

'Will I have magic too, Gander?'

'Oh, most likely. Most likely!' The old man's laugh echoed through the hazel wood . . .

The car turned into the old cemetery of Knockshee. Little knots of old men fell in behind the cortege and followed the hearse to the graveside. Karen stood by the headstone which marked Bessie Hughes' grave and fixed her gaze on the coffin now resting in the grave. The priest recited the final prayers. 'We commend the body of Owen Hughes to the earth . . .' On an impulse, Karen reached down to the mound of soil and scooped up a handful of earth . . .

'Aren't them the grandest of spuds, goslin'?' Gander paused in his digging to lean on the spade. 'God bless the soil!' Karen never ceased to wonder at the miracle that happened each time Gander sliced the spade through the drill and overturned the withered potato-stalks. Six, seven, eight beautiful big potatoes – often more, when Karen dug her fingers excitedly into the warm, moist clay.

Gander lit a cigarette. 'Aye, it's the miracle of life, child.' Karen popped the potatoes into a bucket. 'Soil is life.' He bent down, the cigarette dangling between his lips, took a clod of earth and slowly crumbled it between fingers and thumb.

'Such a beautiful gift from the good God. My father and his father before him worked this same soil and it fed them too. 'Tis no wonder in a way that men fight and die for a piece of land. And in the end of all, it's where we end up – in God's earth, that gave us life. Isn't that only right and fitting, goslin'?'

Karen crumbled the earth between her fingers and let it fall on the coffin below. The priest withdrew and the old men shuffled forward to convey their sympathy to the mourners. 'Sorry for your trouble,' they mumbled with embarrassment. Rough, gnarled hands took Karen's and shook it vigorously. Snatches of hushed conversation came to her in the still autumn air.

'We'll miss him down at The Coney . . .'

'He surely was one for the yarns . . .'

Karen looked across at the little wooded island as it emerged through the clearing mist. Coney Island. The Island of Rabbits. That's what Gander had told her . . .

It was a brilliantly sunny August day when he had first brought her to the island. The slow movement of the oars broke the mirror surface of the lake. Karen trailed her fingers through the water. Gander suddenly stopped rowing and motioned to the girl to look beneath the boat.

'See down there, goslin'! Look hard! D'ye see them?'

Karen shaded her eyes from the glare of the lake's surface and peered through the clear water.

'It's – it's a little roadway!' she cried excitedly as the outline of a series of regular flagstones came slowly into view. 'That's them!' Gander nodded. 'The Rising Stones.'

'The . . . Rising Stones?'

'Aye. The story goes that when the O'Neills had their stronghold on the island, they were protected by the magic power of the wizard from Kylenadree. You see, when the O'Neills were on their way back to their castle, in a bit of a hurry maybe, being chased by their enemies . . .' – he winked at the child – 'didn't the wizard make them stones rise up in the water so that they could run across! And then when the other boys came along, the stones disappeared and the boys disappeared with them into the water . . .'

There was silence as the boat rode gently on the lake's surface before Gander began rowing again. He nursed the little boat among the tall reeds, disturbing several water-birds before beaching the boat on a little cobbled shore. Gander put his arms around Karen's shoulder and guided her through the trees.

'You know, when I was your age this place was mostly grass. The trees have taken over now. We used to come over here – my father and me – rabbit-hunting. The place was alive with rabbits then. That's how it got its name – Coney, Rabbit Island. Oh dear, it's many a year since I had a rabbit stew for dinner. There's no meal tastier . . .'

They fought their way through the thicket until they emerged in a small clearing. Gander gestured toward a pile of stones which was almost entirely covered in brambles and creepers.

'That's all that is left of the O'Neills now,' he said. 'Of course, you have

O'Neill blood in you. My mother was an O'Neill. So our ancestors probably lived here, goslin'!' He drew his long, slender fingers slowly along a large slab of stone. 'And St Patrick used to come over here to pray. So it's a sacred wee place. Holy ground.'

He bent down, loosened a tuft of grass and drew some soil from its roots. He crumbled the soil between his fingers before scattering it among the pile of stones.

'Aye. Holy ground.'

The thud of clay on the coffin woke Karen from her reverie. The grave-diggers had begun to close the grave. Her mother moved away quickly to the car, obviously upset by the sound of earth on wood. Karen felt strangely reconciled by that sound. *Soil is life*. She gave one lingering look before climbing into the back of the car.

The sun had grown stronger, dispelling the last of the mist. The countryside stood out in bold relief, awash in the burnt gold of autumn.

Kylenadree looked resplendent, the tall hazel trees standing stiffly to attention.

'Where are we going now, Mum?' Karen asked.

'There's tea and sandwiches in The Coney Bar for anyone who –'

'Could I go for a wee walk in Kylenadree? I can join you later.'

Her mother was hesitant.

'She'll be all right. Sure, she grew up here,' Uncle Hugh reassured her.

'Well, only a wee walk. And come straight to the Bar.'

'I will.'

Karen clambered over a rickety wooden gate and sauntered down a sloping field to the wood. Entering the wood was like entering a great church. The slanting autumn sun made a stained-glass canopy of the hazel leaves and filtered through to play on the silver bark of the trees. Karen strolled through the wood, savouring its peace. She occasionally paused to listen to the stillness, only to be amazed at the 'music' of the wood – twittering of unseen birds, the drone of insects, scurrying of little creatures, the slow descent of withered leaves. She kicked her way through the carpet of leaves. There was an abundance of hazelnuts scattered among the leaves. She smiled as she remembered Gander's words – 'the source of all his knowledge'.

She had just bent down to pick some nuts when she heard the bang. Short but violently loud. Unmistakably a bomb. It could not have been more than a mile away. Suddenly the music of the wood became discord. Birds fluttered and squawked in terror. Karen flung her arms around a tree and clung to it. The trees themselves seemed to tremble, sending a shower of leaves noisily to the ground. Karen froze to the tree and shut her eyes tight. That sound seemed to course through her blood, freezing it as the sound shot through her body. She had a fleeting image of a sunlit Belfast street. Her mother. She would have to get to her mother.

She had just reached the edge of the wood when the car crashed through the gate – the same rickety gate she had climbed not long before. The car careered crazily across the field and stopped just short of the hedge. Two men jumped out, pulled off boilersuits, balaclavas and gloves and threw them back into the car. One man reached into the boot, took out a plastic can and sprinkled its contents all over the car. In a moment

the car was an inferno. Karen had stood mesmerised by the speed of events and now, when the men turned towards the wood, they saw her.

'Hey! Hey, you!'

Karen turned and ran blindly back into the wood. Branches and saplings whipped her face and body but she kept going. The men had now entered the wood which gave echo to their calls.

'Come here! We won't hurt you! Come here!'

The echo terrified her even more. She staggered onward, clutching her side as she fought for breath. The wood had now become a hostile place. She had become disorientated and ran only where a clear path appeared. She yelped in pain as her toe caught in an exposed tree-root and she fell headlong into a clump of undergrowth. She had to get up – get away – but her exhausted body would not respond. She sobbed fearfully and beat the ground with her fists.

Suddenly Karen felt a calming presence about her. Turning her head sideways, her tear-filled eyes slowly focused on a huge pair of legs, clad in rough hide boots. Her eyes travelled slowly up the enormous body. A tartan kilt, a rough woollen shawl and finally a great block of a red head squatting on very broad shoulders. Karen's eyes were finally drawn to the giant's eyes which nestled amid a wild tangle of bright red hair and beard. His eyes belied his otherwise frightening appearance. They were kindly, reassuring. In his right hand the giant grasped a crude hazel staff. With his other hand he motioned to Karen to come with him. He reached down to take her hand as he looked anxiously in the direction of the oncoming pursuers. The long, lean hand seemed out of proportion to the rest of his enormous body.

Karen found her hand rising involuntarily to take his. He grasped it firmly, hauled her to her feet and in a moment they took off in a crazy, headlong flight. The giant charged through the undergrowth, clearing a swathe as he went with his staff. Karen could not match his great strides and felt herself being half-dragged, half-carried along in his wake.

They left the wood and turned sharply down a narrow, overgrown passageway between two fields. The giant continued to cleave a way through the tangle of overhanging brambles by holding his staff in front of him. Karen tried desperately to stay close to him, if only to shield her body from the brambles that sprang back viciously at her. Unable to match strides with him, she was inevitably lashed by the savage briars that tore at her clothes and hair and streaked her hands with blood until the giant would yank her close to him again. She wanted to scream in pain but no sound would come as she fought desperately for breath.

Just when Karen thought she would pass out from the intensity of her pain, they burst through the bramble wall into a clearing and were confronted by the vast expanse of Lough Neagh. To her amazement, the giant kept running right into the shallow water. From somewhere deep in her throat Karen finally managed to summon a terrified scream – 'No - o - o - o - o!' The giant stopped and stared at her in puzzlement. The expression in his eyes turned to one of appeal, as if he were seeking her trust. Then in a moment he turned, gripped her hand even more tightly, and charged into the water.

Karen closed her eyes, fearing the worst, but an amazing thing happened. The water remained only inches deep, and below its surface she could feel the reassurance of solid broad flagstones. The rising stones! Their headlong charge suddenly became exhilarating, almost refreshing, as the spray from the giant's steps flew up in Karen's face. She found new reserves of energy which somehow enabled her to stay with her protector. And then, in what seemed only a few moments, they reached dry land again. They were on the island. The giant continued through scrub which was waist-high to Karen, to higher ground where he finally paused and turned to watch their pursuers. The two men followed their quarry's path and charged into the lake. In a moment they were floundering in deep water and fighting desperately to stay afloat. Karen watched in disbelief and heard the men's anguished cries for help before she slumped in a heap at the giant's feet.

She awoke to a feeling of warmth. It was dark but a fire nearby illuminated the immediate scene. Karen found herself lying on a bed of withered bracken in the centre of a circle of irregular stones, whose shadows danced crazily in the clearing beyond the circle. She felt a cosy weight across her back and when she sat upright a heavy fleece slid from her shoulders. Slowly the memory of the chase came back to her. She shuddered at the picture of the two men floundering in deep water. Immediately the fleece was draped over her shoulders again. She turned with a start to find her rescuer smiling down at her, his kindly eyes easing her fright. He bent towards her.

A crude wooden bowl rested in his slender hand. Karen took it from him. The bowl was almost full of a steaming stew whose aroma wafted deliciously towards her in the gentle night breeze. The giant gestured to her to sip from the bowl. She brought it nervously to her lips. It tasted exquisite, unlike anything she had savoured before. A long finger pointed to the little joint of meat in the stew. Karen fished it out and sucked the meat from the bone. She relished its succulence. The giant nodded, his eyes sparkling in the firelight.

Karen finished the meal and handed the bowl back to her friend.

'Who – who are you?' she asked. He made no reply except to nod and reassure her with a warm smile.

'But where – how – ?' Again there was no reply but this time the huge figure retreated into the shadows and out of sight. Karen still sensed his presence and felt unafraid. She lay back on the bracken, drew the fleece about her, and gazed into the leaping flames. 'There's no better company than a good fire,' Gander used to say . . .

A searing light forced her eyes open. She sensed a totally different atmosphere. There was noise all about her – noise and cold. Slowly her eyes became accustomed to the light. What seemed a giant bird hovered directly above her, its great talon reaching towards her.

Karen cowered from the approaching menace and instinctively reached for the protective fleece. It was no longer there. She looked around in terror for her protector. Nothing. No fire. No giant. The noise drummed into her head. The light blinded her and all the time the giant talon drew nearer. She threw up an arm to shield her face from the blinding light.

Suddenly a figure dropped right in front of her and a besmirched face looked into hers. Karen gave a little cry of fear and drew back. 'It's all right, love. No one's going to hurt you. It's all right.' The soldier's voice was gentle, reassuring. 'We're going to get you out of this godforsaken place, okay?' Karen sobbed quietly and nodded.

'Now I'm not going to hurt you but I need to get a good grip on you, so Nobby can haul us up. Okay?' He checked his harness then put his arm about her waist. 'Hold on tightly to me, love, and we'll be away. What's wrong with your hand?' Karen shook her head. The soldier shouted to his colleague in the helicopter and slowly he and the girl were winched aloft.

A grey dawn was pouring over Coney Island. As the helicopter door closed, Karen caught a last glimpse of the circle of stones. She could make out the imprint of where she had lain and beyond, what might have been the scorch-marks of a fire . . . The door closed.

'Got a very cold and terrified girl here, Nobby!' the soldier called, draping a heavy, grey blanket around Karen's shoulders. 'Now, let's see that hand, love. A few nasty scratches! Why can't you open it, love? Has it seized up on you?'

Karen looked at her hand in puzzlement, almost as if it didn't belong to her. The soldier took her clenched hand in his and gently prised her fingers open. A handful of hazelnuts fell to the helicopter floor.

GODFREY'S REVENGE

DICK KING-SMITH

I was sitting in the car, waiting for my wife who had a dentist's appointment and, to pass the time, singing to myself the old music-hall song 'With 'er 'ead tucked underneath 'er arm'. Next day I sat down to write a story for The National Trust, and decapitation sprang to mind.

 'Mummy,' said Godfrey. 'Where's Daddy?'

'Why do you ask?' said Godfrey's mother.

'Because I haven't seen him lately,' said Godfrey.

'When did you last see your father?'

'Just before Christmas. What's happened to him?'

'Godfrey,' said his mother, 'I'm afraid your daddy is dead.'

'Dead?' cried Godfrey. 'How did he die?'

'He had his head chopped off with an axe.'

'But why?'

'Oh, stop your endless questions, do!' snapped his mother, and she strutted off to the henhouse to lay an egg.

Godfrey was an unusual chicken. His brothers and sisters ran about the farmyard, pecking and scratching and cheeping and flapping, all in a thoughtless way.

But Godfrey was curious about the world into which he had been hatched. He wanted to know why birds like sparrows or starlings or crows flew in the sky while chickens couldn't. He wanted to know why the farmer and his family all wore clothes while the animals didn't. He wanted to know why the sun was hot and the rain wet.

Godfrey was for ever asking questions. And the question now was – why had his father been killed? Who should he ask? His mother had snapped at him. His brothers and sisters, and for that matter all the other chickens, were, in his opinion, feather-brained.

Deep in thought, Godfrey pottered off down the farmyard. As he reached the pigsties, he saw that in one of them a pig was staring out at him, resting its front trotters on the sty wall. Godfrey looked up at it.

'Excuse me,' he said politely. 'I wonder if you can help me?' The pig grunted.

Is that a yes or a no? thought Godfrey. He tried again.

'You see,' he said, 'my father has been murdered.'

The pig grunted again.

Godfrey sighed. What a stupid creature, he thought. I'll give it one more go.

'The farmer chopped his head off. With an axe,' he said, slowly and clearly. 'I suppose you wouldn't know why?'

The pig gave a huge yawn. Then it said in a bored voice, 'Born yesterday, were you?'

'No,' said Godfrey. 'I'm nearly six weeks old.'

'Ah well,' said the pig, 'you've still got a bit of time left then.'

'Time left?' said Godfrey. 'Before what?'

'Before your head's chopped off too. It will be, once you're big enough.'

'Big enough for what?'

'Big enough to eat,' said the pig. 'Humans eat chickens, didn't you know? Your dad finished up on a plate. Like we all shall, one day.'

'Oh,' said Godfrey. 'Do people eat pigs too?'

'Sure. And they eat cows. And sheep. Haven't you ever heard the well-known expression "as greedy as a human"? Or "as fat as a human"? When I was a piglet and was gobbling my food, my father always used to say to me, "Stop making a human of yourself". He was an awful boar, my father.'

'I never talked with my father,' said Godfrey sadly, 'and now I never shall.'

The pig snorted, with amusement, it seemed.

'Not unless he comes back,' it said.

'Comes back?' said Godfrey. 'What do you mean?'

'His ghost, I mean,' said the pig.

'What is a ghost?' said Godfrey.

'A spirit. The shape of the one who has died, returning to its earthly home. They come at night, and they're usually a ghastly pale colour.'

Like Daddy, thought Godfrey. He was pure white.

'Have you ever seen one?' he asked.

'No,' said the pig. 'Personally, I'm not the type. Some can see ghosts, some can't. Most are terrified by them.'

'But why does a ghost come back?' said Godfrey.

'Because it's sad. And angry. Angry at being sad. So it returns to haunt the place where it once lived.'

'Oh,' said Godfrey. 'I see. Well, thanks for telling me.'

'Don't mention it,' said the pig. 'And I'm sorry about your dad. Just remember one thing, any time you see the farmer with his axe in his hand . . .'

'What?' said Godfrey.

'Don't lose your head.'

That night Godfrey sat on his perch in the henhouse, pondering. Why had his father died? Because humans liked to eat meat and the farmer and his family were humans, so they had eaten his father.

Why, thought Godfrey, must humans eat meat? Chickens didn't, after all – they managed all right without it, so why couldn't humans? If only they didn't eat chickens, then he and his brothers and sisters and his mum would have nothing to fear. If only these particular humans could be persuaded to change their ways. But how?

And at that precise moment, as Godfrey sat wide awake thinking, while all around him in the dark henhouse the rest of the chickens slept, he saw, coming through the pophole, a white shape.

The pophole was closed, of course, to keep the flock safe from the fox, but the shape came right through the wood of the little door, floated through, it seemed to Godfrey, and swam up to land on an empty perch opposite him.

It was the shape of a fine white cockerel – it was the shape of his father, looking exactly as he had in life except for one thing. The proud neck ended abruptly, in nothing. His father, Godfrey could see, was carrying his head tucked underneath his wing.

'Daddy!' said Godfrey softly, so as not to wake the others. 'Speak to me!'

With the tip of its free wing the ghost touched first the top of its neck and then its head.

'You mean you can't speak?' said Godfrey, and he saw his father's beak rise and fall as the head nodded.

'But it is you? I mean, it is your ghost?'

The head nodded again.

At that minute a great idea occurred to Godfrey.

The pig had said that most of those who saw ghosts were terrified by them. Suppose the farmer was? Suppose he got such a shock that he never again . . . !

'Daddy!' Godfrey said. 'Can you make yourself invisible?'

The ghost vanished.

'And then reappear?'

The ghost did.

'Listen then, Daddy,' said Godfrey, and he outlined his plan.

So it was that next morning when the farmer came and opened the pophole door, all the flock hastened out of the henhouse, except one.

Hidden in the straw of a nesting box, Godfrey let out the most awful noise he could manage, the sort of noise, he hoped, that a ghost might make if it still had its head on. It was a kind of a scream and a screech and a squeak and a squeal all rolled into one.

'What the devil is that?' said the farmer, and he flung open the main door of the henhouse and looked in.

And as he looked, there suddenly appeared in the gloom of the interior a fine white cockerel, carrying its head tucked underneath its wing. For a moment the eyes in that head stared unblinkingly into the farmer's own.

Then, as Godfrey watched from his hiding place, his father's ghost floated slowly off its perch towards its murderer.

•

'You should have heard the man shout!' said Godfrey later to the pig. 'You should have seen him run!'

'Wonder what he said to his wife,' grunted the pig.

'Never again! Never again!' said the farmer to his wife in a voice that shook with horror.

'Never again what?' she asked.

'Chicken,' said the farmer. 'We're never going to eat chicken again, none of us, never, do you understand?'

'But why?'

'Never you mind.'

There was a puzzled expression on the face of the farmer's wife.

'You look like you've seen a ghost,' she said.

MIRROR, MIRROR

·

ANNE MERRICK

I am intrigued by mirrors – the illusions they can create, their subtle transformations of reality. I am also fascinated by Castle Drogo in Devon. Whatever ghost might haunt this castle I feel could not be a wicked one. This feeling and the presence of the flawless mirror at the castle were the starting points for my story.

'They've gone off lay,' said Mr Tremlett. 'Old like me and they don't like the cold.'

Bliss withdrew her hand from the prickly hay in the nesting box and smiled at him. Around them the hens clucked and fussed, pecking at the corn she'd scattered. The big cockerel, its tail a cascade of snowy feathers, strutted to and fro.

'He's a proper gentleman,' said Mr Tremlett. 'Letting his wives eat first.'

He opened the gate of the pen and Bliss went through.

'So you're off to Castle Drogo today,' he said. 'And then the pantomime tomorrow. Two treats in a row, eh?'

Bliss nodded. Mr Tremlett ran his hand through his white hair until it stood up like the rooster's feathers. 'We've not seen *Snow White* before have we?' he said. 'And it's one of my favourite stories.'

As they dawdled back up the garden he stopped now and then to pick up a rotten apple or tie back a trailing briar. Bliss loved Mr Tremlett's garden. It was quite different from her own next door. More like an overgrown orchard. Or like the Beast's garden in *her* favourite fairy story; wild, secret, magical, with roses twining everywhere in summer. Mr Tremlett said it was like that because he was too stiff in the joints to look after it properly but she knew that really he liked it the way it was. He always seemed to see things the way she saw them. He understood her better than any of her friends. And he was the only adult who never made silly remarks about her name.

'Typical of your mother,' her father said to her once when she was staying with him, 'to insist on such a name. Serve her right if you turn out to be a real misery . . .'

'But I'm not,' Bliss had said. 'And Mum knew I wouldn't be.'

'Rot!' said Dad. 'How could she? She's not psychic. She's just a hare-brained hippie!'

Made cross by this memory of her father, Bliss frowned and Mr Tremlett said, 'Is that an angry frown or a hungry frown? If it's a hungry one, would you like an apple?'

They had reached the shed where he stored the bins of corn and meal for the hens, seeds and nuts for the wild birds, and the good apples for the winter.

'Golden apple of the sun?' he asked, stooping to peer in through the shed window. 'Or silver apple of the moon?'

Bliss laughed. Side by side in the dark glass she could see their heads, mingled with the swaying branches of the trees and behind them the scudding clouds.

'Mirror, mirror in the wall,' said Mr Tremlett. 'Who's the fairest of us all?'

'Where is this castle?' asked Bliss.

'Near Drewsteignton,' said her mother. 'We're almost there.'

'Good,' said Bliss. 'I like castles.'

'This isn't your usual kind of castle,' said Mum. 'No ruins, no moat, no dungeons. It's modern. The most modern castle in . . .'

She broke off to direct Uncle David who was driving and Bliss leaned back and gazed out of the window. The hills, stripped bare to the bone by

winter, unfolded around them in changing patterns of earth, wood and stone. Letting her mind drift, she thought how comfortable Uncle David's car was compared with Mr Tremlett's which was old and rackety. 'Like me!' he always joked. Mr Tremlett would never talk about his own childhood because, he said, 'It was too wretched to remember.' But he maintained that he took her and Mum to the pantomime in Plymouth each year because it gave him the excuse to go himself, to catch up on what he had missed . . .

'Look everyone,' said Aunt Jane, her crisp curls nodding as she turned to point out of the window. 'There it is. Up on the bluff.'

Bliss saw only a solid, rectangular shape against the skyline before the car swung round a corner and it was gone. Why would anyone want to build a castle nowadays – when there were no barons to quell, no knights to joust, no maidens to rescue . . . ?

'I don't suppose it's even haunted,' she said, 'is it?'

No one answered her. They were arguing about politics again. Uncle

David growing heated because, he claimed, Mum '. . . lived in cloud cuckoo land where money for the poor should grow on trees . . .'

Bliss felt Mum's quiver of hurt and indignation. Slipping her own arm under her mother's she squeezed hard. She'd enjoyed her uncle and aunt's visit but was glad they were going tomorrow. She wanted her mother to herself for a few days.

The castle did not *look* modern. It looked as if it had grown out of the rock on which it stood. From behind its ramparts the winter sun blazed with white fire.

'We'll walk round the gardens first,' said Uncle David, stopping to fiddle with his camera. 'While the light's good.'

Aunt Jane pursed her lips. 'If you start taking photographs,' she said, 'we'll never get further than the garden.'

Taking Mum's hand Bliss drew her away.

'Can I go round on my own?' she asked.

Her mother's bracelets tinkled and winked in the light.

'Oh dear . . . I'm not sure, Bliss . . . what if you get lost . . . I mean . . . hadn't you better . . ?'

They were walking between dense, high hedges of yew that were like green fortifications protecting the castle.

'When we get inside then . . .' said Bliss.

From the woods beyond the garden, rooks rose in a swirl of black wings.

'Well . . .' said her mother. 'Perhaps. But wait until then . . .'

By the time Bliss caught sight of the others inside the castle she had been nearly all round it. She loved the sheer stone weight of the building, its earthen colours, the warmth of its wood panelled walls. Now, as she climbed the stairs to the corridor where the bedrooms were, she saw her uncle and aunt at the far end. They were looking at a picture and did not notice her. Her mother was not with them but from the first room on her left, Bliss thought she could hear the faint, familiar jingle of her bangles. Deciding she didn't want to join any of them yet, she went on and slipped through the second door.

Apart from a tall, grey-haired woman who was in charge of the room, there was nobody else there. The room was large and square. A stone fireplace almost filled the wall opposite the wide casement window. Outside it was growing dark and wall lamps on either side of the hearth cast only a feeble light. In the gloom the beds, with their white coverlets, looked like two drifts of snow. Bliss squinted at a picture of a Welsh lake among mountains, examined the ornaments on the dressing table, wondered why her mother was so long . . .

Moving to the window she looked down. Far below her the ground dropped steeply into a gorge. Billows of mist were rising from the river, filling the valley and drowning the fir trees until only their tops poked through like green brushes. Above the fog the air was clear as glass and the curved blade of the new moon hung sharp against the sky.

'It's nearly time for us to close,' said the woman behind her. 'Are you here on your own, dear?'

Bliss shook her head and said her mother was in the next room.

'Better hurry her along a bit I think,' said the woman.

Bliss didn't move. She was trying to fix the scene outside the window in her memory, like a photograph, so that she could carry it with her and give it to Mr Tremlett tomorrow. The woman clicked her tongue and bustled out into the corridor.

Bliss felt suddenly cold, forlorn, abandoned. Turning quickly to leave she saw a door to her right. Made of the same oak panelling as the walls it was almost invisible in the dim light but clearly it must lead directly into the next room where she had heard her mother. She grasped its brass knob and pulled. The door swung wide and as she leapt over the threshold, hoping to take her mother by surprise, she saw too late that someone was coming through the other way. The someone was moving as rapidly as Bliss herself and, unable to stop, they swooped towards each other. Bliss raised her hands to protect her face. But before they could collide, the air between them solidified. Became hard as iron, cold as snow. Bliss felt her whole body tingle and then freeze as the cold tightened around her, gripping her like a vice. She tried to cry out but the breath was squeezed from her body while slowly, painfully she was drawn, as if through a wall of solid ice, into the room beyond.

When at last the cold released her Bliss stood dazed for a moment. Wayward beams of light from the window, gliding across the polished surface of the wardrobe beside her, seemed to play tricks with her eyes. It was as if she were peering into the room through a dusky veil. Or from a great distance.

'Mum?' she said. 'Are you there?'

There was no answer but from the farthest corner of the room, beyond the great fireplace, she heard a rustle and a sigh as if someone there were turning in their sleep, or just waking up.

'Mum?' she repeated.

There were more sounds of movement and then fear struck her heart like a gong as something came shambling towards her out of the shadows. With a cry Bliss sprang back but even as she did so the wavering light showed her that what had come out of the darkness was nothing to be afraid of – was only a boy crawling on hands and knees.

'Heavens!' she exclaimed, half laughing. 'How you frightened me!'

The boy scrambled to his feet.

'Oh!' he cried. 'I'm so glad you've come. So glad you've come at last!'

He stood where he was, approaching no nearer, and she could see now that he was about her own age. He looked a mess. His shirt had come untucked and hung to his knees over trousers that were raggedly patched. And his feet were bare.

'I've been waiting so long,' he said. 'Waiting ever so long. I thought . . .'

His voice was raspy, as if his throat was parched, and in the drab light his skin, hair, shirt and trousers all looked grey as cobweb. Only his eyes glittered with laughter. Or perhaps with tears. Her fear easing away, Bliss smiled at him. But she was concerned about her mother and worried that the castle was about to close.

'I must go,' she said. 'Everyone will be wondering where I am.'

The boy said nothing but stooped suddenly to pick something up from the floor. As he lifted it, cradling it in his arms, Bliss saw that it was a flat, peaked cap and that nestling inside it, their skins glimmering in the silvery radiance from the sky outside, were three apples.

'Stay a minute,' he said. 'There's something I have to tell you. Something important.'

Bliss hesitated. What could this strange boy possibly have to tell her? She was curious to know but time was slipping by and instead of continuing he stood silent again, running his hand through his hair. She saw a tear slide down his cheek and drop sparkling to the floor.

'I've forgotten,' he cried. 'Forgotten!'

'I'm sorry,' she said. 'I really do *have* to go . . .'

'But I must tell you,' wept the boy. 'It's important. Urgent! Please wait. I'll remember in a minute. Please . . . please . . .'

His gruff voice thinned to a whine as she backed away from him. The high, despairing sound of it filled her head, buffeted her from all around. Closing her eyes she beat the noise away with her hands and as she felt the icy chill of the doorway closing round her again, she heard the one voice disintegrate and separate into the clamour of many . . .

'Bliss. Are you all right? Bliss . . . speak to us . . .'

Opening her eyes, Bliss saw her mother's anxious face close to her own and beyond that the faces of Uncle David, Aunt Jane, and the grey-haired woman.

'She's as cold as a stone,' said her aunt. 'But she's coming round.'

'I'm so sorry,' said the woman. 'She must have walked full tilt into the mirror. I'd closed the door on it thinking there would be no more visitors.'

Bliss felt her mother's arms encircle her, smelled the warm musk of her clothes. Struggling upright, she tried to tell her about the boy on the other side of the door. But all her mother said was, 'Don't fret, darling, and don't try to talk. There's only the mirror behind the door. You knocked yourself out trying to get through it!'

'The mirror's fixed to the back of the cupboard between the two rooms,' the woman was saying to Uncle David. 'It's flawless you know. So perfect that people don't see it's there and we usually keep a chair against it to warn them . . .'

'D'you think you can walk, Bliss?' asked Mum.

'Yes – but Mum I can still hear . . .'

'I really am so sorry,' said the woman again. 'I think you should bring your car right to the castle door . . .'

Uncle David departed and Aunt Jane, calling for him to wait, scurried after him. Supporting Bliss along the corridor and down the stairs, her mother soothed, comforted, explained away her fears as the after effect of shock. But all the way through the castle – and even when they stepped out onto the drive – Bliss could hear the boy hammering on stone, scratching on wood. Pleading with her to wait. To listen.

Throughout the night Bliss tossed and turned. Every time she dropped to sleep the boy was there again. He cried to her from the shadows of her dreams, insisted there was something he had to tell her. Something she *had* to hear. When at last the morning arrived she staggered out of bed, haggard and heavy-headed.

Downstairs the house was more chaotic than usual. Everyone had slept late and her uncle and aunt, who had wanted to leave early, were already packing their car. In the kitchen her mother was distracted. The toast had burned, the milk not yet arrived. Bliss sat down at the table and watched Mum sawing fiercely at the misshapen loaf.

'You'll cut yourself,' she warned. 'Let me do it.'

Her mother flung down the knife and Bliss began to cut neat, even slices. While she worked, she told her mother about her dreams, trying to explain about the boy and his message, about her feeling that she *had* to go back – today – to Castle Drogo . . .

'Castle Drogo?' cried Mum, rescuing melting butter from under the grill. 'We only went there yesterday! That bang on your head must have frazzled your brain!' And before Bliss could argue Uncle David came into the kitchen with the milk.

Bliss picked at her breakfast, moped between upstairs and downstairs, said goodbye to her uncle and aunt and then crept out to see Mr Tremlett. At least *he* would listen to her. But when she knocked and pushed open his back door, she could see him dozing in his chair by the stove. Hoping he might wake she waited a moment. Now and then he gave a little groan as though something in his dreams troubled him. The blanket she'd made for him out of knitted squares had slipped to the floor. Picking it up she laid it softly over his knees before going out again.

She tried to put the boy out of her head but later that morning as she glanced in the mirror in the hall, she saw not her own round face looking back at her, but his – the pale skin, the ravelled hair, the glittering eyes.

'Please,' he whispered as she covered her eyes. 'You must listen . . .'

Mum was cramming sheets into the washing machine when Bliss told her she was going to spend the afternoon with her friend, Sally. She did not like lying to her mother but could think of no other way. And because she hardly ever lied – and frequently spent time with Sally – Mum did not question it.

'Oh Bliss, no . . . I'd rather you . . . I mean . . . remember we're going to have tea with Mr Tremlett's sister in Plymouth before the pantomime.'

'Oh Mum! That's ages yet!'

'Well, I suppose . . . perhaps . . . but keep an eye on the time. Make sure you're back *early*.' She gave the faulty door a thump to start the machine. 'Four o'clock at the latest!'

Bliss thought there would be plenty of time but the bus meandered from village to village and by the time she left it at Drewsteignton, it was already well past two. On foot the castle driveway seemed very long. And the weather was changing. A strong wind harrying clouds out of the north brought an aching cold. Against the stormy sky the castle looked black and grim as a prison. As she reached the gatehouse, a flurry of wind spattered her coat with white flakes.

'You've left it a bit late,' grumbled the man at the desk as he took her money. 'Won't have time to look round properly before we close!'

Bliss, however, didn't pause to look at anything. Dodging among the straggling visitors, she darted from drawing-room to dining-room to kitchen, up the winding staircase and on along the corridor to the mirror room.

There were two people in the room as well as the lady in charge. To her relief Bliss saw that it was a different woman from yesterday and that the door to the mirror stood wide, with a chair set against the glass. She stood very still and listened for the boy's voice. The visitors were whispering together and in the chimney the wind fluttered and piped like a trapped bird. But otherwise there was total silence. Bliss stared into the mirror. She saw only herself – and the room behind her, dim and brown, the only light among its shadows shed from the whiteness of the bedclothes.

The visitors were talking to the woman in charge and together they drifted towards the door to the corridor. Bliss spread her hands across the mirror's surface and closed her eyes. There was no tingle. No gripping cold. For a moment nothing at all happened. Then the murmur of voices in the corridor faded and she felt the glass ripple gently away from her as though she were lowering herself into a pool of quiet water.

Opening her eyes Bliss saw the room exactly as she had seen it yesterday: empty, distant, blurred with dust. Under pressure of the gale outside, the window suddenly rattled and snow whitened the panes. But here, on the far side of the mirror, there was warmth. And a sense of such peace that the knot of fear inside her unclenched and melted away.

'Boy?' she said.

No answer came. She knew now there would be none. Stepping back she glanced at the floor and saw, gleaming at her out of the dust, a single golden apple. And piercing the apple – like a heart impaled by an arrow – was a long white feather, its plumes flickering in the draught. As Bliss picked up the apple it crumbled to powder in her hands. But the room was filled with its fragrance. Sweet as roses. Sharp as sorrow.

Bliss stood in the telephone booth in the village square and with frozen fingers fumbled for the change in her pocket. Outside, in the light spilling from the kiosk, snowflakes whirled and danced. They made her feel dizzy, disconnected from the world. She sniffed, wiped her face on her damp glove, and inserted ten pence into the slot. It was five o'clock. Mr Tremlett had wanted to set out for Plymouth soon after four and she was still here, miles away in Drewsteignton. But then – *that* must have been what he had intended.

Far away she heard her mother pick up the telephone.

'Mum?' she said.

'Bliss! . . . Bliss wherever are you? I've been searching *everywhere* for you . . . ringing Sally . . . all your friends to try to . . . Bliss you are very naughty!'

The words were cross but her mother's voice did not sound cross. It sounded tight, thin, its music flat.

'I'm sorry, Mum. . . . But I had to come to Castle Drogo . . . I told you I had to . . .'

'To Castle . . . Drogo . . .' Her mother's voice was scarcely above a whisper. 'You're at Castle . . . ?'

'No,' said Bliss. 'I'm back in the village now. Waiting for the bus. But Mum . . . what about . . . what about Mr Tremlett?'

There was a long pause while the figures on the telephone panel ticked steadily down.

'Bliss . . . come home. There's something I have to tell you but I can't . . .'

'I know,' said Bliss. And her stopped-up tears flowed.

'Bliss, you can't *possibly* know . . . Look, you must. . . .'

Bliss heard her mother talking about Mr Tremlett but could not focus on what she was saying. She found one last ten pence in her pocket, and as she put it in the slot, the white feather in her hand trailed against her cheek like a caress.

'I didn't tell him I couldn't find you,' said Mum. 'I simply told him you were held up . . . and that we'd take the train and join him at the theatre . . . so he went ahead on his own . . . But then something . . . it was starting to snow . . . and his car . . . something happened . . .'

Her voice died away altogether and Bliss said, 'I know, Mum. It's all right. Really. That was why he . . . why the boy . . . wanted to warn me. Because if we'd gone with him . . .'

The figure on the panel was down to five. She heard her mother gasp and then say, 'I don't understand any of this . . . When I went to tell him about you being late he said . . . it was almost as if he *knew* where you were . . . he said he'd grown up in Drewsteignton . . . that his father was one of the labourers working on the castle . . . and that he used to go up there himself sometimes.'

So that was why, thought Bliss. Of course!

Two pence to go. In the distance she could hear the rumble of the bus climbing the hill.

'And once . . . one night,' her mother went on, 'he was locked in. Trapped in a space between two unfinished rooms . . .'

'Yes,' said Bliss. 'We'll talk when I get home. Must go, Mum . . .'

She had time to hear her mother cry, 'I'll meet you, darling!' and then the money went.

Looking into the snow-speckled dark, Bliss saw her own face in the glass and for the briefest moment watched it quiver, change – and the sharp, thin face of the boy smiled in at her.

'Just wanted to tell you,' he whispered, 'that you're the fairest of them all! Be happy as your name . . . Bliss . . .'

The snow fluttered round him like feathers, enfolded him like wings. Brushing her lips with the rooster's feather, Bliss pushed open the door of the booth and went to meet the bus.

THE THING IN WAITING

JOAN AIKEN

This story, like most of mine, did not arise from one single incident, but from a whole series of cross-fertilizations: visits to two different houses, the National Trust's Oxburgh Hall in Norfolk and Stokesday Castle in Shropshire (not owned by the Trust); a statement in a TV programme about gardening that some plants were considered so precious that, when sold or given away, they would be despatched with a special guardian to tend and watch over them; also a reference to the Fens, in a historical essay, as 'the back door of England'; and finally an allusion to The Old Man of the Mountains, in yet another piece of history. This mysterious character, leader of the Assassin Sect, has always appealed to me, and the idea of making a connection between him and the back door of England was not to be resisted.

Mind you, I blame what they call 'the media'. All them newspapers, telly and radio programmes, *Who's New, Up Your Way*, local interviews, gossipy chat shows and feature stories with a smitch of this and a touch of that. Weren't there all that rubbish blown and poked and dribbled into folk's ears, nobody betwixt here and Land's End would ever have heard of our part of the country, nor about Orris Place, nor Lady Elfrida's Christmas lily. We'd ha' stayed quiet and comfortable, not thought of nor visited, like we been for the last nine hundred years.

But there you go. Once a person – or a place – turns into News, they don't rightly belong to theirselves any longer. And that's bad. That can be terrible sad.

Orris Place weren't all that big. Nor it weren't writ up in a lot of guide-books, because it were main okkard to get to, even the quickest way to Orris lies all along of our little twisty roads through the marshes, roads that seem to career right, left, and rat's ramble, and can take you miles out of your journey, given you don't know which exact turn to take at every little crossroads. The signs all tell different stories. Place names come and go as if the sign-makers just meant to befoozle strangers. There's a rhyme said in our parts:

> Criss-cross east
> Five at least
> Criss-cross west
> Half the rest
> Only one
> Leads straight on
> And that will wind
> Out of mind
> Afore your journey's done.

Pretty fair jabber, it be. Unless you know where to start from. Or where you aim for.

It's said there was allus a big gentry house on the site at Orris Place, since long before Roman times. And the history folk, them as know, could point you the various bits that were left from one bygone time or another. Part of it was big old square blocks of stone, that's from the Romans, they allus left their mark tidy and workmanlike. Then there was a part standing on legs, that was put up by Saxons, who chose to keep the cattle under-neath and sleep warm and dry up above. Then the Normans dug a moat and put up a chapel and builded a tower. Main fond of towers, they Normans. Then King Henry Eight, he added on a wing, and Good Queen Bess, she clapped on another, and Queen Anne, she stuck on a fourth side. So it ended up as a square, with a cobbled courtyard in the middle, and the moat running round outside.

A real mishmash, you might say, a bit of this and a bit of that. But not big. No, the whole place not much more than a tidy, sizable farmhouse with a tower at one corner. And a little old pantry-size chapel next the tower.

Along the side of the chapel, a row of heads. Inside the chapel, the tomb of Sir Alured Hamley, who died at the Fall of Antioch, in one o' they Crusades. His widow travelled out next year and brought back his corpus, and afore that she voyaged on to Jerusalem and out beyond, so 'tis told. 'Twas from that journey that she brought back the lily, along with her husband's bones.

She was a learned lady, so the tale goes, knew a deal about herbs and medicines, could talk to you in Latin and Greek and they Eastern lingoes. It's said she did a power of good to the folk in the fens and marshes, a fair-dealing landlady, gave money and food for a plenty charities. One story has it that when she was out in the Holy Land, she went to visit the Old Man of the Mountains, Hasani Sabh, or Rashid ad Din – some say one, some say t'other – so as to hold learned conversation with him. And while she was there she was able to cure the favourite one of his hundred sons, who was lying mortal sick of a fever. In return for her saving the lad's life, the Old Man gave Lady Elfrida this lily bulb. And he told her that it would go on living and flowering for a thousand years, so long as one of her family was still alive to tend it, in the place where it was planted.

Well, be that how't may, there allus *has* been some of the Hamley family at Orris. And the lily's allus bloomed, regular as sun-up, at Christmastide. Not on Christmas Day, but at the first stroke of midnight on Christmas Eve.

Seen it? Oh yes, I seen it, plenty times. Just a tiddy small flower, it were, not one of your big, gaudy, show-off blooms, but a thin stem with flowers up it, about the size of a lily-of-the-valley. The colour was enough to burn your eyes – a deep, deep ruby red. And the scent! It crept on you like smoke, and put a kind of wonder into your mind, enough to make you remember things that never did happen. And then 'twas gone, in a flash.

You could travel half the world over, and never find another like it.

How come I seen it? My dad and I would mostly be at Orris around Christmastide, staying in the Queen Bess wing, where there was allus rooms for workers on the estate. Stone-cleaners, we are, see. Leastways my dad passed away, nine years come St David's Day, but I still keep up the old trade. There's not so many of us left, now. Travel round the shire, we do, from one big house to another, a-scrubbing of the stonework and statuary, a-scraping off the moss and lichen, repairing, repointing, making all newlike and vitty. There's many a big old mansion fine and square-standing this day, that would ha' been all scrumbled away, or covered up in moss and ivy, 'tweren't for me and my dad and others like us. Stone is like skin, it needs care; only lasts a few centuries longer than skin, 'less you look after it. 'Tis a good life, faring about the shire, sleeping a week or two here, a week or two there. Suits me. I like to think while I work. Night-times, in some cool, ancient stone-walled sleeping-loft, I like to read. Read what? Why, the Scriptures, o' course. There's enough in that book to last a man his natural life.

Anyhow, that's how I first come to see the Orris lily, on a fine frosty Christmas, dunnamany years back, when Dad was still in his prime, and I was a hopeful young 'prentice, my rheumaticks didn't chaw on me like they do now. (That be the dread bane of our trade: it do come from keeping still, hours together, in some okkard spot, perched up a ladder all stiff and twisted and stretched, no way to move, scrubbing and scrubbing away at some old stone gargoyle. That's the way all your bones and sinews get pulled out of true, clenched amiss, and 'tis mortal hard, after days and weeks passed so, to unclench 'em again.)

So, as I say, this Christmas feast found us at Orris. The frost had held for weeks, all the marshes, mud and reeds, was friz over. So was the moat round the big house, clear marble-green ice right down to the mud bed at the bottom. And the thorn trees likewise. All beyond the moat and across the marshes there's a multitude o' those, blackthorn, buckthorn, hawthorn, every kind o' thorn. And in this winterlong frost they was all furred over wi' white, and shone in the sun like filigree.

I spoke of the row of heads along the side of the chapel. Sir Alured was the first, and his wife Lady Elfrida alongside of him. And the rest was more family. Sir Alured's grandson got to be a baron, and *his* grandson got to be an earl. But they kept the name, never changed it. Then the title died out, for the earl's son was killed in some battle, and he had only a daughter, but she married a cousin, so there was still Hamleys in the house. The heads was put up later, sixteen hunderd or so. They took the likeness of Sir Alured offn his tomb, and that of Lady Alfrida from the portrait at Waldey Abbey. (She gave money to the monks there to have masses said for Sir Alured's soul, as he died in battle, no time to be shriven.)

The minute I saw Lady Elfrida's face, I thought: you're the lady for me. And I cleaned her up main careful, with my sponges and cleaning fluid (that was a secret 'twixt Dad and me. Every man in the trade has his own secret.)

'Twas a handsome, strong face, with flowing hair under a little circlet, and deep-set eyes. Mouth half smiling but firm. Looks like she'd take no aggrification from anybody. That was the best part of my work. I felt a kind of closeness between her and me, as if I recognized her. And she recognized me, too. 'I'm your man, missus,' I told her.

After that, every Christmas when I come back – 'How's it been, then, this year, Lady Elfrida?' I'd ask her, in my mind, like; and she'd look back, calm and friendly, and answer me in her own way. She cared for her folk, were they grand or simple, if they belonged to the place.

Down below, alongside the chapel, under the row of watching heads, that's where the lily grew. (Course the heads weren't there when she planted the lily, they was put up later.)

There was a little stone-walled 'closure, about the size of a chicken-run. Very snug and sheltered, 'twas, caught the sun all day, and screened from our north and east winds, which do come cutting and whistling here, straight from that old North Pole. That was the corner where Lady Elfrida set the bulb the Old Man of the Mountains had given her. Likely she had the wall built round it, special. And that's where the lily stayed for the next nine hundred years, or as near as be bothered. (Fine, black, tilthy soil we have hereabouts.) 'Tis told that Lady Elfrida used to feed the plant with dried blood; ox-blood that'd be, mostly, for it was all ox waggons here in those days. Anyhows, the plant throve, and spread, and prospered. But grow in any other spot it would *not*. If a bulb was broke off and planted elsewhere, if one was given to a friend or neighbour, it would always pine and dwindle away.

Queen Bess when she came to stay here, with the Hamley of that day (Earl Maurice, I bleeve) you may reckon that she was fair wild to have a bulb, and they gave her one, of course, you can't say no to your liege Queen, but 'twas no manner of use. She took it away with her, and fed it on dust of gold and pearls, likely, but it died.

My first Christmas at Orris, Mrs Hamley came to me and my dad, as we was a-cleaning up the rows of saints around the chapel doorway, and she says: 'You'll dine with us in the Hall tonight, Mr Wragby, and your son too, of course?' We said we'd be proud to.

That was what was allus done, at the Hall; Christmas Eve, all the folk that worked on the estate – cowmen, smiths, ploughmen, woodmen, shepherds, masons – were all bidden to the big Hall (that was in Henry Eight's wing) for Christmas Eve dinner. Like a Harvest Festival dinner, 'twas, only with Christmas puddens and pies. Mrs Hamley, the Mrs Hamley of our day, was one o' the family too, and had married her cousin. She was a short, stocky lady, not the way I think of Lady Elfrida. But she had a straight eye and a keen look to her, upright, old-fashioned; and a friendly word for all there, knew their children, down to the last new-born. And her husband, that was also her cousin, Mr Gervas Hamley, he were a friendly-spoken, handsome old gentleman too, but ailing with a murmurous heart. Had to be wheeled in a basket-chair.

After the dinner, and after we'd sung 'For they are jolly good fellows' and a tidy few Christmas carols besides, all the people moved out into the courtyard. There we stood waiting, quiet and regardful, along by the Queen Anne wing, that my dad and I had just been cleaning.

I noticed Mrs Hamley look at her watch and then at the chapel clock, anxious-like. (The yard was all lit up with lanterns and flaring torches.)

She said something to her husband, and he shook his head.

'They're a-worrying about young Mr Edward,' Mr Macgregor, the head gardener, told my dad. ''Tisn't the first time he's cut it fine.'

Mr Edward was the son, supposed to be studying science and medicine at Cambridge College, but, by all accounts, he was a wild young spark and spent more time than he ought up in London, playing cards in gambling clubs with some havey-cavey friends, when he should 'a been studying his books.

But anyway, when the hand of the chapel clock was creeping on towards midnight, we begin to hear the sound of a motor, way off, across the marshes, and – wonderful fast, considering 'tis a bitter old night, and the winding roads all slippy with ice – that motor comes roaring over the moat bridge and in under the arch, where no tradesman is ever allowed to drive. And what a motor we see – a big, long-snouted open-top racing job, wheels like pumpkins, and all its tubes on the outside, that made enough roar for the Day of Judgment. No doors to it, young Mr Lordly just steps over the side, in his gloves and goggles.

'Did you think I wouldn't make it, Mother dear?' he says, laughing, careless-like, and Mrs Hamley she says, 'No, no, of course, dearest boy, we knew we could rely on you,' and old Mr Hamley in the wheelchair, he coughs and gasps out a Christmas greeting to the lad. But his face was drawn and gloomy, and I thought as I looked at him: you poor old gaffer, you're not long for this world. And maybe glad to leave it.

For Mr Mcgregor had told my dad that already Mr Edward's debts and doings were a heavy weight and trouble on the old man.

Well, we all move in around the little old stone-walled penfold where the lily grows. During the daytime 'twas covered with a big half-transparent waterproof sheet, to guard it from the weather and any dust that might blow about from Dad and me cleaning the stone round about.

I've allus been a tall gangly one. Which is right useful in our trade, for I've a long reach, and, with my brushes and cleaning sponges, can get to corners that a shorter chap could never stretch to.

So – besides not wishing to seem pushful – I'd stayed at the back of the crowd, sure enough that I could see over folk's shoulders, when it came time for the lily to bloom. And I saw two things.

The crowd of estate people had left a space, a pathway, between two groups, so that Mr Hamley in his wheelchair, and his wife and son, could move straight to the low wall, only knee-high in front, that was round the lily pen. And now, as it come to midnight, they moved slowly along that path.

Mr Edward pushed the wheelchair, and I happened to glance sideaways at his face when he was a-passing me. And the look on that face turned my blood almost as cold as the marble-green ice in the moat. For it was black with discontent, with grudge, and sour-mindedness, and boredom.

I could see that, for two ha'pence, he'd yell out with annoyance and spite, that it drove him wild to be obliged to come back home, year after year, and take his part in this ancient fuddy-duddy practice, which, plainly, he saw as something left over from the Stone Age, something only suitable for kids, and yokels, and doddering old nincompoops.

I wondered how long he would go on putting up with it, if that was how he felt. But perhaps he was obliged to.

Then I looked back past Mr Edward, across the middle of the courtyard. And there I saw a mighty queer thing.

There's that story in the Scriptures that I like to read every while or so. About Lot's wife. How she looked back at the doomed city and got changed to a pillar of salt. From the very first time I read that tale, I had a clear notion of what a pillar of salt would look like. And in the middle of the Orris courtyard, now, I saw what looked to me like the ghost of a pillar of salt. A bit taller than me, 'twas, and no special shape to it, just tall and thin; taller and thinner than a tall, thin man would be, if you take my meaning; and, furthermore, I could see clean through it, to the stonework and mouldings on the Queen Anne wing that my dad and I had cleaned that morning.

There it stood. Or hovered.

Now I heard a long-drawn-out breath, an 'Oooooh!' of wonder, and turned to see that, as the chapel clock clanged out the first stroke of midnight, so Lady Elfrida's lily had bloomed. And the crowd begins to move forward, slow and civil, each pair giving way to the next, for a short, fond study of the bloom. Nobody outstayed their turn, but you could see that each pair, after they looked, was sad to trudge off and give up their place. Dad and I took our turn, and smelt that wonderful scent, delicate and spicy both, that seemed to blow from beyond the other side of the globe.

Then we shuffle onward, and, not long after, are both in our beds in Queen Bess's wing.

'Dad,' I said, 'did you notice a kind of a *thing* in the middle of the courtyard, time the lily bloomed?'

'Kind of a thing, what kind of a thing?'

'A kind of a misty column – like, say, the ghost of a statue.'

But no, he hadn't.

'Get off to sleep now, boy,' he grumbled. 'Too much Christmas ale! Your mind be full of moonshine.'

Next day I chanced to be at a job of cleaning on the portico of the old garden temple, alongside of Mr McGregor, who was working on a hedge nearby. So I mentioned the matter to him. (No, I'm telling a lie, not next day, which was Christmas, and a holiday, but the day after. Those times, folk took no account of Boxing Day.)

'Mr McGregor, is there any tale about a kind of a thing that might be see'd in the courtyard, time that lily blooms?'

Mr McGregor gave me a slant look, over his pruning hook.

'You saw it, did you? It's not all that can. I can myself – being Highland born – and Mrs Hamley can – but there's a deal of folks wouldn't know what the pize you were talking about.'

'What is it, Mr McGregor?'

'The family call it the Waiter,' he said. 'So Mrs Hamley, she told me.'

'The Waiter?' I thought of a chap with a tray, and a napkin over his arm.

'Summat that's waiting,' said Mr McGregor. 'I reckon it's been waiting ever since Lady Elfrida first brought back the lily. Come to these parts *along* of the lily; to guard it, you might say. To watch over it.'

That made sense. There had been such a powerful feeling about that shape: watchful, unflagging, biding its time.

'Some of they big, grand plant-nurseries,' Mr McGregor said, 'that sell foreign species, young trees, plants that's real rare and precious, they won't let one o' their stock go without there's someone at the other end that's qualified to care for 'em. And if there's nobody, why then they send out a qualified person, till the tree, or whatever it be, is well bedded and settled in.'

Well, that made a kind of sense, too. But *for nigh on a thousand years*? The Old Man of the Mountains, I thought, must have had a great regard for his lily.

After that, I allus used to take a look in the lily pen, going and coming. Once the red flower was gone by – it only bloomed for a few hours – there was little to see: just a mess of spiky leaves. Lady Elfrida's stone face looking down from above.

Now and agen, come we was at Orris over Christmastide, I'd see, in the middle of the yard, what, in my mind, I'd come to call the Thing-in-Waiting. It never budged from its place, and few but me ever seemed to notice it. Just sometimes I'd notice a body give a queer, puzzled glance as, maybe, they brushed clean through the silent, patient, shape, or past it. Myself, I'd never do that. I kept a decent distance, like you would from a sign that says *Danger, High Voltage*.

Well, times went on, and times got worse. Poor old Mr Hamley, by and by, he took and died, and the Orris estate got run down; land was sold off, workers were laid off. Mrs Hamley came sadly to Dad and me at Christmas and said, 'Mr Wragby, I'm feered I can't afford to ask you to come any more, after this year.'

'Ma'am, I'd do the work for nowt,' he says, very shocked; but that she won't have.

She looked thin and pale, all shrunk away, like a little owd withered leaf. I'd never ha' thought that a stout, well-fleshed lady, as she did use to be, could wane and shrivel so, in a few years.

'There's bitter trouble atwixt her and young Mr Edward, now he's got a position up in London City,' Mr McGregor told Dad and me. 'He's got this smart young lady-friend now, Miss Vondra del Mayo. One o' they journalist females.'

'Yes, I heered of her, I bleeve,' Dad says. 'Seen her on television.'

'Very like. She's on telly more than she's in her own bed, by all they say. And she writes for various o' they shiny magazines, *Yours* and *Hers* and *Ours*; special for one called *Patrimony* or *Symposium* or some such, all about furniture and pictures and fashions in summerhouses.'

Mr McGregor picked a snail off the bush he was pruning and dropped it in a pail of salt water. I reckon he'd have liked to do the same with Miss Vondra del Mayo.

'What she and Mr Edward want is to have Orris Place open to the public. He says that'd make a sight of money, pay off all the debts; and *she* says, "'Tis a shame that such a grand old place is not available to the man in the street".'

'The man in the street'd never find his way here,' I said. 'He'd end up down on the sea shore.'

'But what about Mrs Hamley?' Dad asked. 'What does she say?'

'She's sot against any such notion. She says owd Mr Hamley'd turn in his grave. And, what's worse, Miss Vondra del Mayo is keen to have one o' they telly programmes come and film the lily when it flowers. "So," she says, "the whole world can share in this wonderful epiphany."'

Fine words, young lady, I thought. But maybe there's some things as the whole world is not meant to share. Some things is supposed to be kept small, to each group of folk for their own.

'What does Mrs Hamley say to *that*?'

'She can't abear it. I hear her shout out, "Over my dead body!" – they was in the Yew Tree Walk, and Mr Edward getting right nasty about it. "You do realize, Mother, you are turning your back on thousands of pounds?" he says, cold and drawly. Seems that's the fee they offer. "And I've had dozens and dozens of requests from newspapers and magazines. News of the lily is getting about." "Turn my back?" Mrs Hamley cries out. "I wish I could turn my back on you two for ever. I'll not allow it! And that's my last word. You know what it says in your father's will."

'Seems in Mr Hamley's will he left orders forbidding any such thing, unless his widow was to give permission. And it's plain she never will. But just the same,' Mr McGregor went on, 'stories are starting to be printed in magazines about the Orris Place lily. "England's Secret Treasure", they call it. I reckon Miss Vondra del Mayo is at the bottom of it all.'

So, times went on, and times got worse. My dear old dad died. Then I read in the paper that Mrs Hamley, poor lady, she had a stroke. Not long after that, I read in another paper about her funeral at Orristhorne All Saints, and how she was to be laid to rest in the chapel at Orris Place, alongside Mr Hamley.

Humph, I thought. Now's your chance, young Master Edward.

And, sure enough, he took it.

The house was thrown open to the public. Next thing, there's new signposts all across the marshes, with a little drawing of a mansion house inside of a lily flower, and a hand pointing, and 'Orris Place' lettered up big in fancy lettering.

I didn't go there to see.

I'd no fancy to see all the world and his missus paying their three-pound entrance fee, and then a-peering and a-gawking at those things I used to take such care of – Lady Elfrida's head and Sir Alured's tomb.

But, come next Christmastime, I got an invite.

'We are reviving the fine old custom of inviting all those connected with the Orris Place estate to come and be present at the flowering of Lady Elfrida's Lily, which will also be shown on North Sea Television,' said the printed card. 'Drinks and a buffet supper will be served in the Henry VIII Hall from 10.30 p.m. on Christmas Eve. Admission £30.'

Well, I ask you!

Pride would ha' kept me away, anyhow, but, as mischance 'ud have it, I'd lately given my back a nasty jar, a-falling off a ladder at Frisby Castle, and so was stuck abed.

I telephoned Mr McGregor (these days he was working for the Duke of Colchester) to ask if he'd be at Orris Place, but he said no, wild horses wouldn't drag him. ''Tis a wicked shame what's happening at Orris,' he said. 'Mr Edward got married last autumn to Miss Vondra, and now they plan to open a Theme Park, and a waxwork show, and a bingo hall, and an ice rink. They reckon all that will be funded by the fee they receive for the TV viewing of the Christmas lily.'

Come Christmastide, flat on my back though I was, half shamed at my own inquisitiveness, yet I could not keep from switching on the programme. I was wishful to get a last view of Lady Elfrida. And that I did.

First they showed a distant view of Orris Place and its moat. That must ha' been taken weeks before in autumn-time, red berries on the thorn trees. For now 'twas bitter cold again, iron-hard frost all over the marshes.

Then we saw the thorn trees, guarding the place like prickly ramparts.

I thought of the Ancient Britons, and the Romans, and Saxons, all the folk after them, who had lived in that place and called it home.

Then we had a shot of King Henry's banqueting hall, and the guests all guzzling down their thirty-pound Christmas dinner.

'It looks warm and festive in here,' the commentator told us. 'But outside the temperature is bitter cold, ten degrees below freezing. Even the River Fleme is solid in its bed.'

Then we saw the customers gathering in the courtyard. Not quiet and reverent, as in Mrs Hamley's day, but all bustling and excited, little kids, mums and dads, young couples laughing and joking, happy to be asked what they had to say, and none of them *did* have much to say, beyond what a big thrill this was, and such a different Christmas from last year, when they were at Auntie Sharon's.

Then we saw young Mr Edward and his lady. She'd been a brunette, but she'd turned auburn since I last saw her on TV.

He was saying, 'Of course, I myself have been present at this ceremony ever since I was a small child.'

Yes, I thought, and how sour and bored you were. How you wished you could get the blazes away from it all.

'Now,' he went on, 'we are so glad to share it with all these friends. And, in future, we hope to share it with many, many more; for the lily is to be taken and propagated by an expert from the National Arboreal Institute of the United States of America. We are going to divide the bulb and so permit many, many other friends to enjoy this unique experience. The main bulb will be in California, where it will be tended most carefully by Professor Courney Hansell Window, the great American orchid expert. We are sad to lose it, naturally, but Professor Window will soon be sending us back off-shoots from the parent bulb; and what he gives us for it will be sufficient to put the Orris Place estate back on its feet again. Professor Window will tend the bulb just as well as the Hamley family have done here.' He glanced up at the clock and finished quickly, 'So here we say goodbye to the Orris lily for a few years. But we are sure that it will thrive in its new home.'

The camera moved up to the row of heads above Mr Edward. I saw Lady Elfrida looking down. Goodbye, my dear Lady, I said to her, inside my own mind.

I had heard a few gasps from the crowd, as they took in what Mr Edward was saying. And my own breath seemed to have stopped.

Now the camera moved down again, focusing, close-up, on the lily, and we saw its tiny, blazing-red petals begin to spread, as the clock tolled out its first stroke.

And then, suddenly, there was a flash, and a lot of confusion. The screen went blank.

'Excuse me,' said the lady back in the studio, 'we seem to have lost the picture. I'll transfer to another camera.'

And then she cried out in amazement, 'Good heavens, one of the stone heads has fallen right on our camera!'

The picture came back, but it was pitching about, people were running and shouting and screaming. Another of the heads could be seen falling. Sir Alured this time.

'I'm afraid Mrs Hamley has been hurt,' gulped the lady commentator. 'Oh, my goodness!'

Now the picture showed us all the big yard at Orris, the crowd lurching in confusion. But, in the middle of it all, I could see the Shape, white and misty, calm and motionless.

Then it began to move, silent as a cloud passing along. Straight across the space it steadily went. Young Mr Edward turned, and I could see that he saw it advancing towards him. I could not hear the scream he gave – the sound was lost – but I saw his mouth open wide. Then he was whirled up in the Shape and carried clean through the chapel wall, and out of view.

Then the lady said, 'I am so sorry, there seems to have been some kind of interruption to the Lily Festival at Orris Place, we are returning to the studio.'

Next day I read in the paper about how they only just got the guests out of Orris Place before the whole building went up in flames. No one knew what could have caused this, the insurance company was fair mystified, for the fire seemed to have started everywhere at the same single moment – chapel, tower, east, west and south wings all blazed up like a barrel of tar and sawdust. Not one stick left to stand on another. The stonework all reduced to black, powdery dust, Lady Elfrida as well as the rest.

And the lily? Not a shred left, not a leaf, nor a petal.

But here's a queer thing.

Mrs Hamley – Vondra del Mayo that was – she'd got killed by Lady Elfrida's head falling on her. And Mr Edward, *he* was found, bedded *deep* down in the frozen moat. Nobody could understand – then or after – how he could have got underneath all that ice, solid marble-green to the bottom.

However he'd got there, dead as a mackerel, he was.

But away across the marshes from that spot, they found a *path*. As if something – something wonderfully hot and fiery – had passed along through the frosty thorn trees, a-melting and a-withering. And the grass was all browned and burned, like as if a hot fire-engine had passed that way. All across the frozen marshes, so far as the coast, that straight, burned path took its way. And, on the sandy sea-shore, it was lost.

Which way did it go? Why, eastwards. Back to the Old Man of the Mountains, I reckon.

THE DORABELLA VARIATION

ALICK ROWE

In his famous Enigma Variations, *Sir Edward Elgar included a musical portrait of his groupie Dora Penny. Elgar lived for a period of his life in Malvern, where today much of the surrounding countryside is owned by the National Trust. He once told a friend not to worry if, after his death, he should hear somebody whistling a tune on the Malvern Hills because 'it'll only be me'.*

Dora couldn't stand much more. She took a deep breath and tried to concentrate on the hills through the car window but the argument in the front seats hammered relentlessly to and fro like a tennis rally. The trip to Worcester had not been a success and the return to the hotel was turning out worse.

Her mother said, 'You *must* work. If you don't put in the hours, what's the point in us coming here?' (Fifteen-love, thought Dora.)

Leo replied, 'You don't write. You know nothing about writing.' (Fifteen-all.)

'What do you mean? I teach writing. English literature is my subject!' (Thirty-fifteen.)

'You don't teach writing. You teach the kids how to *criticize* writers and if you think that's the same thing, you're a fool!' (Thirty-all. This was going to be a nasty game.)

'If I'm such a fool, how come I'm paying the bills at the hotel?' (Forty-thirty.)

'I've offered to go halves.' (Deuce. Dora groaned inwardly.)

'What with?' (Advantage Caroline. Let it go, Leo, she begged silently.)

'Is money the only thing that matters to you?' (Deuce.)

'Without it you wouldn't be here.' (Advantage Caroline.)

'Maybe I should leave.' (Deuce.) 'I can get very bored with your negativity.' (Advantage Leo.)

'You can be so hurtful!' (Deuce.)

'*I* can be hurtful? What about you?'

Dora screamed.

Leo turned, startled, and her mother slammed on the brakes and swung round in the seat. 'What's the matter, darling? Do you feel sick?' Dora tugged at her seat-belt. 'Yes,' she muttered. 'Sick of you t-t-two . . .' Dora struggled to untangle belt and words and force her tongue into the right shapes. 'Going on and on-n-n an d-don.' Actions spoke louder than words. She opened the back door and got out. Leo murmured 'Oh, for God's sake,' and Caroline wound her window down. 'Dora! Where do you think you're going?'

Dora turned back to the car and tried to yell back that anywhere would do so long as it was out of the car – but it didn't work so she stamped briskly up the hillside. 'Dora!' her mother called again. Leo's eyes were closed. 'Let her go,' he said. Caroline swung on him. 'Don't tell me what to do with my child.' Leo opened his eyes; they watched her climbing determinedly uphill towards the ridge. 'She's fifteen, not a child,' he said and Caroline nodded slowly. On that at least they agreed.

Dora strode across the ridge, relieved to be out of sight. The misty day prevented much of a view but Dora was impressed by the stillness and silence. She wandered down to a small copse where she stopped and listened for any sign of life. She felt a need to be still and was slowly sitting on a fallen tree when a voice – very dry and precise – spoke to her in the centre of her head, exactly as if she were wearing her Walkman. 'If we are perfectly quiet,' it said, 'perhaps someone will come and talk to us.'

Dora sat very still. She had no idea what the voice meant or where it came from. She was surprised not to feel afraid and was wondering what on earth was happening when she was startled by the arrival of a robin on the branch of a tree just to her right, cocking its head at her and shuffling its stalks of legs. Dora found herself smiling. There was a movement near her feet as a fieldmouse darted from the mouldering leaves. Another strange thing happened. Dora was suddenly aware of a slight warmth along her right side from shoulder to thigh – as if somebody had sat very close to her on the trunk of the fallen tree.

Enough was enough. She jumped to her feet and strode determinedly out into the certainty of the afternoon. As she hurried back up to the ridge, not sure whether she was frightened or not, another sound came into the centre of her head. Somebody was whistling a gentle, lilting tune. She shook her head as if to dislodge it but it persisted and both she and Caroline yelled in shock as they almost collided on the hilltop.

'For God's sake!' she panted. 'Where were you? I was getting worried.'

Dora stared at her. The tune in her head had ceased. 'What?' she whispered absently.

Caroline shook her head. 'You live in a world of your own!' she said as they stamped down to the car.

Dora liked the Wellingtonia Hotel. Although it wasn't very big she imagined it was like staying in a country house. Caroline had chosen it – the very place for Leo to get over his Writer's Block and finish the novel. Dora wasn't exactly sure what a Writer's Block was since it was a taboo subject. She only knew it was something to be got over – like measles.

She wandered over to the piano in the drawing-room. Mother and Leo were upstairs and the other guests had finished tea long ago. She opened the lid and hesitantly began finding the notes of the strange tune that had come into her head. She had given up piano lessons long ago but had a good ear. Now she almost had the tune. She put down her cup on the polished top and concentrated.

'Dorabella.'

The voice wasn't in her head. She turned quickly. One of the waiters was smiling at her. 'Yes?' she said cautiously.

He was confused. 'Sorry?'

Now Dora was confused too. 'What did you say?' she demanded.

'Dorabella. The piano.'

She didn't know what he was talking about and snapped down the piano lid to cover her embarrassment so that it crashed loudly, embarrassing her even more. She walked haughtily towards her jacket ignoring the young man.

'The tune you were playing,' he explained patiently, carefully polishing her ring of tea from the glossy piano with his cloth. 'You know. Edward Elgar.' He loaded his tray with crockery and carried it towards the door.

'What's your name?'

He turned, surprised. 'Robert. What's yours?'

Dora didn't reply. 'What do you mean "Edward Elgar"?'

He stared at her incredulously. 'There's somebody in Malvern who hasn't heard of Edward Elgar? He wrote that tune you were playing.' She shook her head, too amazed to feel stupid. 'It's called "Dorabella". He used to live in Malvern.' Robert grinned. 'You didn't tell me your name.'

Dora felt all the early signs of a stutter and tried hard to fight it. 'W-where is he now?' Robert shook his head in further disbelief as a voice shouted his name somewhere and he hurried through the door. 'He died in 1934,' he called back. She tried to tell him her name was Dora but the stutters took over and anyway he was gone.

Dora left the hotel bike behind a low wall and began walking uphill. She didn't know what to expect. The best explanation was that she'd imagined it; that was what everybody else would say. She decided to stay five minutes. If a robin or mouse turned up she might stay longer.

The clearing in the copse was exactly as it had been yesterday and she sat very still on the tree, fearful and hopeful. She glanced at her watch: two and a half minutes had gone. Birds called and wheeled above the branches but there was no sign of her robin. Four minutes. She scanned the dead leaves for a fieldmouse. 'I'm h-h-here,' she whispered, feeling silly. She looked at her watch and sighed. Five – four – three – two – one. She stood up.

'Dorabella!' said the voice in her head.

Dora abruptly sat down again and the voice chuckled. Almost immediately there was a fieldmouse nibbling at one of her boots and a robin dancing close to her head. She had worked out what to do and talked back in her head. That way she would avoid the stutters. 'My name isn't Dorabella.' The voice laughed. 'I know that. Come on. Up you get. No dawdling. There's a track just behind you. Don't tread on the mouse.'

They emerged from the trees overlooking Worcestershire and Herefordshire and Dora gazed and gazed, feeling his approval of her wonder. 'You used to live here,' she murmured.

'Had a house in Malvern – it's demolished now. And there was Birchwood Lodge,' the voice explained. 'Turn to your left.' Dora obediently turned to overlook another lovely stretch of farms and pasture land. 'Little group of houses down there,' the voice went on. 'Village called Storridge. See? Birchwood's close by. Peace and quiet.' Dora felt she could have stayed there all morning but the voice was suddenly impatient. 'Come on. Let's get you back safely to that boneshaker of yours. Dorabella liked a good long bike ride too, you know. That silly young girl once cycled to Birchwood from her home in Wolverhampton just to see me. Forty miles!'

Dora retraced her steps, glad that there were no other walkers nearby.
'Where are you staying?'

'The Wellingtonia Hotel.'

'Never heard of it.'

Dora described its whereabouts but there was no sense of recognition until she mentioned the huge tree outside the hotel which provided its name. The voice rang loudly in her head with a kind of triumphant snort which stung slightly. 'The giant redwood tree, otherwise known as Wellingtonia. I know where you mean. Down by the Colwall Road. Used to be a house called Wychcrest. Went there once to lunch.'

Now she was walking the ridge above the wall where she had left her bicycle. 'Whoever Dorabella was,' she said quietly, 'you must have really liked her.' There was no quick reply but Dora felt warmth against her arm and could imagine somebody very close. 'Pretty young thing – just like you,' the voice said softly in her head. Dora chose her words carefully. 'I've never seen a ghost.' The voice took on a mockingly sinister tone. 'Oh, I'm a truly terrifying sight! Off you go now. Come to Birchwood tomorrow. I'll see you there.'

The familiar tune came gently into her mind as she began walking downhill to her bike and she had a superb sense of feeling very special. A sudden thought struck her and she turned. 'Were you famous?'

The whistling abruptly stopped and the air turned chilly. 'I beg your pardon?' She could not tell whether he was genuinely annoyed or making fun of her and thought she had better play safe. 'S-s. Sorr. Sorry,' she said aloud. There was a long pause and she thought he must have left her. 'Well, I'll be damned!' he said eventually. 'Dorabella had a stammer too.' The wave of good feeling swept back over her and she began running down to the road. The voice come into her head as if from a great distance. 'You can hear it in the music,' it called. 'Dorabella's stutter. You be careful riding back to Wychcrest!'

Her mother was fretful and tired. 'Where have you been?' she said, hurrying to meet her. 'Nobody in the hotel knew where you'd gone. Go straight up to Leo.'

Dora found him pacing up and down, his six o'clock vodka and tonic in his hand even though it was only quarter to. 'Your mother is in many

ways a clever and perceptive woman but she just doesn't understand!' He took a swig from the tumbler and gazed out of the window. 'Understand what?' asked Dora timidly. He turned. 'Me. You. Writing. Everything. Do you know what I mean?'

Dora felt both that she did and didn't but she realized this was no time to disagree. He knocked back his vodka and went to the wardrobe where he kept the bottles. 'Do you think it's The Age Thing?' he asked as he refilled. Dora was shocked. The Age Thing was also taboo: Leo was almost ten years younger than Caroline. Dora knew she had better get her response exactly right. She shrugged expressively. 'Exactly,' Leo said, handing her a vodka and tonic. She didn't much like alcohol but the gesture of equality deserved a good response so she flashed him her best smile. He sat on the bed and patted the space at his side. Dora sat – but not too close: ghosts were one thing, frustrated writers were another. He laid an arm across her shoulders and swivelled her so she was watching their reflections in the wall mirror. 'Look,' he said. 'There's a far bigger gap between Caroline and me than between the two of us.' As far as years went it wasn't true and Dora said so. 'Look,' he insisted. 'We are youth.' He got to his feet, swaying slightly, and wandered back to the window. 'Next time you see Caroline,' he muttered, 'look at her. Closely.' Dora hated this disloyal talk but when Leo turned he had tears in his eyes. 'The loneliness of the artist,' he said very softly. 'She doesn't understand.' Dora was impressed to see a man cry and when he smiled bravely through his tears and held out his arms to her she obediently went to be hugged and they stayed like that for a while, swaying slightly and trying not to spill their drinks.

'So how has the book progressed today?' she asked brightly, hoping to hear good news. He looked tragic. 'It hasn't,' he said. 'Not a word.' Dora gave him a quick kiss. 'You'll finish it. I know you will,' she said, 'and it will be wonderful and make you rich and famous.' Leo smiled and stroked her cheek. 'Thank you,' he said. 'For your youth and beauty and your belief in me. Off you go now. I can work an hour before dinner.'

Dinner was, as usual, good and the mood that went with it was – unusually – even better. Leo had rethought a problematic chapter and only drank one glass of wine, keen to get back to it, so all three were mellow and relieved. Robert was on duty in the dining-room which added to Dora's feeling of goodwill and, after coffee, when Leo had gone upstairs to work and her mother had left for a chamber concert in Malvern, she hung about in the sitting-room.

'Was this place always called The Wellingtonia?'

Robert straightened magazines on a side-table. 'Expect so. Why?' Dora shrugged. 'Just wondered.' He put the last of the brandy glasses on his tray. 'What are you doing now?' he asked carefully. 'Only, I'm free in about half an hour if – you know – you wanted to go for a walk or anything.' She carefully counted five seconds so as not to seem overkeen. 'I d-don't mim. My. Mind,' she replied, annoyed at finding the stutters intruding, and hoping like hell it was their final appearance that night. Robert didn't seem to notice. 'See you by the tree at nine.'

They met at eight fifty-five and sneaked out of the back gate. 'I've found out what the house was called before it was a hotel,' he grinned. 'Wychcrest?' Dora suggested. Robert put an arm round her. 'You're full of surprises!'

Dora learned he was eighteen, came from Northampton and was an engineering student in his first year at Manchester University, earning much-needed cash as a waiter during the holidays. He was easy to talk to and the stutters kept a respectful distance. It was almost dark by the time they returned to the hotel and separated to different doors. 'You're a respected guest; I'm just a lowly waiter,' he laughed.

Two minutes later, in Dora's quiet room at the end of the corridor, Robert was able to inform her that the hotel transport wasn't due back for an hour and that one of his colleagues had taken Leo a pot of coffee twenty minutes earlier and reported him hard at work, and unlikely to leave the room.

Robert produced a surprise of his own. He had been flicking through one of the hotel's books on Elgar for something to interest Dora and had come across a head-and-shoulders photograph of the woman the composer had nicknamed Dorabella. The caption gave her real name – Dora Penny; she had been twenty-two at the time of the picture.

Dora Penny and Dora White were strikingly alike – strong features, full dark hair and prominent arching eyebrows. 'It's you,' Robert said quietly. Dora took the book and gazed at it disbelievingly. The nose was different and you couldn't tell what colour the eyes were from the black and white page but they were definitely dark like hers. Robert held up a tape cassette. 'Also Elgar's *Enigma Variations*,' he said triumphantly. Dora looked up questioningly. 'Variation number ten,' he explained, 'is the Dorabella music. It's ready to play at the right place.' She took the tape with such excitement that Robert was more impressed than ever. 'So what do I get for all this research then?' he asked, and they were still kissing when the hotel minibus brought the Malvern concert party back, forcing him to leave quickly, quietly and with great reluctance.

Caroline didn't stay long. 'Thank you for what you said to Leo earlier,' she yawned. 'It absolutely did the trick.' She kissed Dora. 'I wish I could jolly him on in the same way but – let's face it – I can't. Perhaps it's The Age Thing.' Two taboo references in the same night; Dora was astounded. Her mother turned at the door and winked. 'We're a great team,' she smiled. 'Sleep well.'

The moment Dora heard her mother's door close she slotted the cassette into the Walkman and propped the book open at Dorabella's picture against the bed's headboard. She sprawled on the bed, eyes riveted to the page and switched on.

There it was. As Elgar had intended it. Orchestral instruments wove the whistled tune into a revelation. Dora stared at the photograph, unsure if the pretty mouth offered a rueful smile or a pout of disapproval. *Variation Ten* came to an end and Dora wound it back.

This time she walked round the room in the way the music told her Dora Penny would walk – precise little steps, trying not to make a noise. A cello sang sweetly before other strings intervened, posing a problem, but those unstoppable little steps fluttered them away. Dora was dancing now, moving softly across the carpet. The strings introduced a new complication – stronger this time – but they made no difference; the irritating fussiness was invincible. Dora had the sudden feeling that Dorabella must have been a pain who would have hated her right back.

Dora danced *Variation Ten* a third time, singing too, quietly at first, all the time turning this way, that way, as the music dictated. She closed her

eyes and tried to see in her mind's eye not a head-and-shoulders Dorabella but a full-length young woman, slim, in long skirts, sleeves and tiny
black boots – she was sure they would be tiny – but Dora Penny obstin-
ately refused to appear. She rewound the tape yet again, the volume high
now and digging into her head. She sang louder and covered the floor
with those fluttering, stuttering steps, turning left, turning right, turning
left, turning right, turning left, turning . . . and her half-closed eyes
snapped wide open as shadowy figures smiled and tapped time. The
music turned her left, turned her right and Dora tried to stop but
couldn't. Everything was different. The music was different – a piano was
playing *Variation Ten* alone. Another difference: Dora no longer in jeans
and shirt but dressed as she had been trying to dress Dora Penny. She had
the uncomfortable feeling that since she had not been able to lure Dora
Penny into her room at The Wellingtonia, Dora Penny had removed Dora
White . . . but where?

Very upright in a high-backed chair a short lady, rather plump, was

watching her with a bland, stony look while at her side the pianist, middle-aged, with a large moustache and thinning hair, smoked a cigar. He smiled at her and raised his eyebrows. She knew she was seeing Edward Elgar. 'Dora!' shouted Caroline. 'For God's sake!'

Dora snapped off the music and tried not to look at her mother in the doorway. 'What do you think you're doing? You're singing – if that's what it can be called – at the top of your voice and it's half-past eleven! Have you gone quite mad?' Dora would have liked to offer some explanation but there wasn't one. 'Sss. Sor. Ssor,' she stuttered. 'I should hope you are,' snapped Caroline. 'Now bed, if you please.'

When Dora knew Caroline would safely be bewailing teenage craziness to Leo, she quietly opened her door and put the book about Elgar on a table in the corridor. She didn't intend to share a room with Dora Penny.

Dora stopped in the lay-by outside Storridge church and consulted Robert's sketch-map before crossing to the Birchwood road directly opposite. The possibility of a limerick arose – 'There was a young lady of Storridge' – but she gave up immediately.

Soon she swung right and found herself greeted by a friendly pair of border collies behind a high wire fence. Dismounting, she pushed her fingers through the mesh, smiling and talking, and the voice exclaimed:

'There was a young lady of Storridge.
Who would only eat parsley and borage.'

Dora laughed out loud. 'Now say goodbye to our friends and look to your left,' the voice said. 'There's Birchwood Lodge.' She gazed at the small pebble-dashed cottage at the end of the lane. 'Wrote some of my best work there – including that damned variation of yours!' The little house had been enlarged quite recently but felt warm and friendly. 'Look behind you,' the voice murmured. 'What do you think of that?' Dora turned and saw the rounded summit of the Malvern Hills. 'That's the Worcester Beacon. We'll go up there one day.' A row of conifers screened off much of the view. 'Damn cheek!' snapped the voice. 'They wouldn't have planted those firs in my day!' Dora nodded, believing it.

She stretched out in the sun and munched an apple. 'What do I call you?' she asked. No answer; she tried again. 'What did Dorabella call you?' The reply was matter-of-fact. 'She called me "His Excellence".' Dora grimaced. 'That's gross.' When the voice spoke again it carried an edge of pomposity. 'It is no such thing. She was a very polite young woman . . . unlike certain others bearing her name.' Dora grinned. 'I shall call you Edward.' She felt his disapproval surprisingly strongly. 'If you don't mind,' the voice said stiffly, 'I should prefer Sir Edward.'

Dora nearly choked on the apple and sat up. 'You're a Sir? That's impressive.' She felt the disapproval melt into a smug silence. He was conceited; he reminded her of Leo.

'Leo?'

Dora had forgotten he seemed able to read her thoughts and explained. Sir Edward politely kept silent but she felt he was not terribly impressed by her descriptions of the man or his work. 'He gets terribly depressed,' she said.

There was a sudden sadness in the air. 'All of us feel that sometimes. All of us who take the game seriously. Composers, writers, artists. Other people try to help but it's a lonely business.' Dora nodded. '"The loneliness of the artist". Sometimes Leo cries.' She felt his urgency like stiff breeze. 'Then you must cheer him up. That's what Dorabella used to do for me. But never intrude. Sometimes the loneliness leads to great work.'

Time passed. She heard whinnying from farm stables and an aeroplane droned lazily across the sky. Dora had listened to the *Enigma Variations* on the way to Storridge and thought a lot of it lonely and sad, particularly the beginning. The colours of the trees burned bronze. Sir Edward sounded quiet and subdued. 'Time to go.'

Dora climbed over the gate, and hauled the hotel bike upright. 'I saw you last night, didn't I?' she asked carefully, to cheer him up. Sir Edward gave nothing away. 'Did you?' he teased. 'Can you be sure? What did I look like?' Dora described the pianist. 'Sounds a damned handsome fellow,' Sir Edward insisted. 'Do you think he had an eye for you?' Dora wasn't sure how proper it was for a ghost to flirt and Sir Edward was delighted. 'Hoighty-toity!' he mocked. 'I'll see you tomorrow!'

Dora rang her bell and cycled to the Storridge road. As she turned left a very faraway voice called,

'There was a young lady of Storridge
Who would only eat parsley and borage.
She cooed as she chewed
This ridiculous food
And preferred it to kippers and porridge.'

Dora screamed with laughter and put on her Walkman to hear the tape again as she began the long haul back to The Wellingtonia where – though she could not know it – tempers were frayed. Leo's work had not gone well and Caroline had received a shock at the bank when she had checked her balance. Dora was also late for lunch.

'You!' Leo yelled across the dining-room to Robert. 'Bring a bottle of Côte du Rhône.' Robert nodded to show he had heard and continued serving a guest with her main course.

'If you drink wine now,' protested Caroline hopelessly, 'you won't get anything done this afternoon.'

He accepted the challenge. 'So where's Dora?' (Love fifteen.)

'How should I know? I thought *you* were Big Buddy at the moment.' (Fifteen-all.)

'Now you're jealous of your own daughter. That's sick.' (Thirty-fifteen.) Caroline sipped at her water and Leo saw his chance for an easy point. 'What a mixed-up mess you are, Caroline.' (Forty-fifteen.)

'Maybe my daughter has found someone her own age.' (Forty-thirty.) Leo lined up his winning shot. 'Which is exactly what *I* should be doing.'

Caroline put down her napkin and pushed her chair from the table. 'Excuse me,' she murmured, trying not to hurry but wanting to be out of the room before he saw the tears in her eyes. Game, set and match, Leo thought and snarled triumphantly at Robert. 'Are you deaf? I ordered a bottle of Côte du Rhône.'

Dora knocked at her mother's door and went in. 'Hello,' she said cautiously. Robert had told her about the scene at lunch. Caroline put down her book. 'Have a good ride?' she asked. Dora nodded. 'Should I find Leo and cheer him up?' Her mother laughed without humour. 'Don't waste your time.' She turned to face Dora. 'How do you feel about going back to London?'

Two days earlier Dora would have jumped at the chance. Now she was not so sure. She had two new friends – a waiter and a dead composer – as well as a mission to keep Leo's spirits as high as Dorabella had kept Sir Edward's. She shrugged. 'I don't know.' Caroline studied her face. 'Well, think about it.' Dora nodded and left.

Caroline sighed. Maybe Leo was right; maybe she was jealous of Dora's youth and optimism. Her eyes briefly rested on his table near the window, chaotic with pages. For the first time she faced up to the fact that maybe Leo hadn't got enough talent or determination after all. She refused to cry again and picked up her book instead. She didn't know where he was and didn't care.

Dora ate alone in the dining-room and enjoyed playing the politeness game with Robert. 'Thank you, Robert.' 'Not at all, Miss White. Will there be anything else?' 'Not at the moment, thank you, Robert.' 'Thank *you*, Miss White.' Robert whispered, 'See the ladies in the corner? You've got to meet them. I'll fix it over coffee.' Before she could ask questions he had gone.

Charlotte and Catherine Tilsley were eighty years old and their mother had known the Elgar family when they lived in Malvern.

'Oh yes. Mother knew them well – as well, that is, as anybody was allowed to,' Charlotte smiled thinly. 'Did they live in Malvern all their lives?' Dora asked. The ladies laughed. 'Dear me, no. They began their married life in London.' Dora was shocked. She gazed at Catherine. 'But I thought he loved the countryside.' 'Well, so he did, dear, but it didn't stop him living – where was it, Charlotte? Just off the Cromwell Road somewhere? Then Norwood. Oh, and they spent ten years in Hampstead, too.'

Catherine held out her cup and Dora refilled it uneasily; this did not fit Sir Edward's image. 'After Alice's death he took a flat near Buckingham Palace.' Charlotte also held out her cup. 'He would enjoy that,' she muttered dryly. Catherine smiled. 'He came back to this part of the world for his last years but by then he was far too grand to bother with the Tilsleys. Would you pass the cream, dear? Thank you.'

The sisters were catty but enlightening and Dora waited for more. 'His poor wife,' sighed Catherine. 'Alice Elgar was cut out of family wills for marrying below her, you know.' She smiled and nodded to a group of departing guests. 'But Edward Elgar had a knighthood,' Dora protested. 'Yes, dear,' Catherine patiently replied, 'but it only returned her to the class from which he had removed her.'

Charlotte picked up her bag and reached for her stick. 'Oh, I think Alice knew what she was up to. She met a good-looking piano teacher, saw his potential and took her chance.' Catherine leaned in confidentially. 'She was ten years his senior, dear, and not altogether a beauty. Still, without her money and encouragement Mother always thought Edward would never have amounted to much.' Catherine agreed. 'Before their marriage and after her death he wrote nothing of any value. He was totally reliant on her.' 'And then on Carice,' Charlotte put in. She saw Dora's puzzled face. 'His daughter,' she explained.

Dora stared. 'I never knew he had a daughter.' Charlotte leaned in confidentially. 'It was all too easy to forget the fact.' 'Poor girl,' Catherine said. 'Poor girl,' Charlotte echoed. While they fussed over the bill, Dora asked what Alice had looked like and gulped as they told her. She knew now who had watched her dance from the side of the piano.

At Reception Dora ran into Leo, hair dishevelled and face chalky. He looked terrible. Dora thought he might be drunk. 'Pretty little Dora,' he grinned foolishly. 'Just what I need to cheer me up.' Without my mother this man would be nothing, she thought, and fixed him with the sort of glare she imagined Alice Elgar would have used. 'Tough,' she muttered and hurried upstairs. The book was still on the ledge and she had already finished the first chapter when Robert tapped gently on her door. She showed him the picture of plump, tiny Alice Elgar, stony-faced and sad.

Wrapped against the autumn drizzle in a plastic mac, Dora stood at the fallen tree and furiously berated Sir Edward. She had stayed up half the night to finish the book, getting more and more tired and angry. He seemed not to understand how he had offended.

'You called your daughter Fishface in public,' she accused, horrified.

Sir Edward chuckled. 'She did look rather like a fish.'

'And you sent her away to boarding school.' Sir Edward was bewildered. 'Only just up the road.' The voice grew lofty.

'Great music was expected of me. I couldn't be disturbed by a clumsy child.'

'In the *Enigma Variations* why didn't you write a variation for Carice?'

There was a brief pause. 'Don't be ridiculous!'

'What's ridiculous about it?' persisted Dora. 'You wrote one for Dorabella.'

Sir Edward was beginning to tire of the game. 'Altogether different. Dorabella was useful to me.'

Dora was furious. 'That's the trouble. You use people. You liked Dorabella just because she gave in to you all the time, never contradicted you, always did what you wanted. Yuck! All that secret flirting!'

Leaves moved on the floor of the clearing and branches shivered in a sudden breeze. A roaring in her head made it ache. 'I beg your pardon,' Sir Edward thundered angrily. 'How dare you!' Dora fought back. 'How dare *you*? Didn't your wife ever object?' The roaring in her head increased and leaves swirled round the clearing. 'HOW DARE YOU!' The robin did his best to hang on and Dora refused to be scared. 'I bet there were times when she felt really hurt.' '"*She*"?' Sir Edward snapped. 'If you mean Lady Elgar, kindly have the courtesy to say so. If not, shut up! You,' hissed the ghost of Sir Edward Elgar, 'are not like my darling Dorabella at all. I was wrong. I have been cheated.' 'I notice you didn't think twice about putting your darling Dorabella's stutter into your music,' Dora added. 'And just exactly how do you know so much about Dorabella?' She paused before replying. 'Because you are a great master and your music describes her wonderfully,' she murmured humbly.

The swirling agitation settled and the twitching face of the fieldmouse thrust through the leaves. Dora took her chance and pressed on. 'Composers and writers play on the fact that they're special and need special treatment but they're not. You're just the same as anybody else.' There was a disappointed silence before Sir Edward at last complained petulantly, 'But I believed you understood. Don't you remember? "The loneliness of the artist"?'

'Yes,' shouted Dora, infuriated, 'and I damn well know *why* they're lonely. It's because you think only of yourselves. It's because you're all unbearable!'

Branches suddenly thrashed, catapulting the robin out of sight and cartwheeling leaves buried the mouse. Dora took a few staggering steps,

scared and screwing up her eyes against flying dust and foliage. It was like being caught in a whirlwind and, at the centre, she thought she saw for one brief moment the faint outline of a man wildly brandishing a walking stick but then she was out into the light and running, her head full of loud sardonic music she would not identify until – three years later – she heard the Demons' Chorus at a Proms performance of Elgar's *The Dream of Gerontius*. The mocking music crashed furiously behind her eyes, knocking her off balance so that she tripped and fell heavily. When she had slowly hauled herself to her feet, whimpering and winded, the nightmare noise had left her and she limped gingerly down to the bike, really scared for the first time.

Robert was raking leaves from the lawn when he saw Dora wobble up the drive. He yelled to a colleague to fetch Caroline and ran to help her.

'How are you feeling now? Better?' Caroline smiled down at her daughter who looked very pale, young and vulnerable propped up on pillows.

Dora nodded. She could not tell her mother what had happened and had lied that she had taken a fall from the bike. A pleasant doctor had examined her and pronounced nothing worse than a strained knee and ankle – and of course she was shocked. Dora felt shocked all right. She felt scared, too – and confused. Why was all this happening to her? Was it all imagination? Her mother laid a cool hand on her brow and Dora closed her eyes. 'I've told Leo you and I are leaving after the weekend,' she said. 'This has all been too much for you and I should have realized it. He's going this afternoon and wants to say goodbye to you. How do you feel about that?' Dora shook her head and her mother nodded briskly. 'I'll say goodbye for you.' Dora opened her eyes. 'But what about his book?' Caroline kept her smile. 'I don't care a damn about his book. I doubt that there will ever *be* a book. *You're* my main concern at the moment. Now what about a light lunch? Could you manage scrambled egg?' Dora had been sick earlier and did not fancy the idea. 'Would it help if I asked Robert to bring the tray up and stay for half an hour?' Caroline asked innocently. Dora's eyes slowly opened and for the first time that day a slow smile spread over her lips. Caroline leant to kiss her and walked to the door. 'Mum?' Caroline turned. 'What about – you know – about you and Leo?' Her mother saw that it mattered and signed her lover off with a cruel epitaph. 'Writers are like tiny children,' she said. 'Very charming but very selfish.' Amen to that, thought Dora. 'Also extremely disappointing,' Caroline added to herself, closing the door.

Robert brought scrambled egg, small smoked salmon sandwiches and a half-bottle of Muscadet. 'I don't like alcohol,' Dora murmured. 'I know,' he replied shamelessly, pouring it, 'but I do.' He sat on the side of the bed and kissed her softly. 'Now eat,' he said firmly, reaching for a sandwich. 'Afterwards I want to know what happened. You said some weird stuff earlier,' he added gently.

Dora told him, hardly daring to look at his face. It took some time, thanks to the stuttering, but he kept his brown eyes on hers, nodding and silently encouraging when she stumbled. When Dora had finished he got slowly to his feet and she gazed anxiously at him. 'You don't think I'm crazy?' He took a deep breath and looked down at her. 'Oh, yes,' he said seriously.

'Sure you are – but no more than the rest of us. Where's the Elgar book? I need to do some reading.' He finished the last of the Muscadet, kissed her again and took the tray downstairs. Dora felt very sleepy and soon dozed off.

Next morning, Robert borrowed the chef's Renault to drive Dora as close to the copse as possible. She was uneasy about the venture but trusted him and felt too feeble to argue. It took all her determination to limp up to the ridge.

In the silent copse Robert took Dora's hand and she looked round nervously. 'I've braw brought a f-friend to meet you,' she called aloud. Nothing happened. She glanced at Robert who smiled encouragingly. 'Sir Edward?' There was no movement and the only sound was a distant tractor. Nothing happened. Robert suddenly turned and, holding her very tight, kissed her so long and hard that she almost suffocated. It was the most passionate and longest-lasting kiss Dora had ever experienced and when at last Robert took his mouth from hers she collapsed on the tree gasping for breath and desperate for the robin or the mouse, afraid of what Robert would think if nothing happened at all.

Nothing happened at all. 'That's it then,' said Robert confidently. 'It's all over.'

Dora believed him. She felt a mixture of emotions: relief certainly but also a sense of loss. 'I don't understand,' she muttered. 'What's wrong?' He stroked her hair. 'Remember the book? Remember the last time Dorabella visited the Elgars? She took her fiancé with her. That was the end of that.' Dora nodded slowly. The visit must have been proof that Dora Penny was growing up to a life of her own and would never be his own darling little Dorabella to play with again. Dora didn't know whether to feel happy or sad. Robert gave her another kiss, gently this time. 'Say goodbye. We've got a lot to do. We've got to pack your mother off to Notting Hill and work out your schedule.'

Dora stood very still. 'Goodbye then, Sir Edward,' she said in her head. There was no response.

Robert slipped an arm round her waist and they gingerly set off. Robert wondered what Dora had seen in the clearing – to be honest he wondered if she had seen anything at all but it didn't matter. Dora White was beautiful, interesting, fun. She had been sick and worried and now, he hoped, felt better. Moreover she was going to stay on to work at the hotel for the last ten days of her holiday. Things could be worse. They clung together and stumbled downhill. Robert decided he had a lot to thank Sir Edward Elgar for.

Back in the deserted clearing a robin suddenly hopped onto a branch as a deep voice thoughtfully hummed the Dorabella variation and a field-mouse surfaced from the sea of leaves.

A Lady in Blue, Unidentified

TERENCE BLACKER

I first walked among the living dead in the British Library while researching a novel. Later, in the middle of winter, I paid a visit to Oxburgh Hall in Norfolk where something really rather unusual happened to me . . .

I write this report in the library of Oxburgh Hall, the agreeable late-medieval moated house in Norfolk where I have been a guest for these past four days. By the end of this week, I am confident that my task will be complete.

The vampires will be dead.

No, please don't be alarmed. I shall not, in these pages, be taking you into the spooky world of heeby-jeebies and hobgoblins. It is the *myth* of the vampire that I am here to slay – the farrago of fictional nonsense (fangs! long cloak! crazed blood lust!) that shall be destroyed by the oldest weapon known to man.

Reason. Logic. Our old friend, common sense.

Because, although I earn my living from writing books for children (for telling tales *in* school, as it were!), I am essentially a man of fact.

So, when the National Trust invited me to contribute to this volume, challenging me to disprove the existence of vampires at one of its properties, I was tempted. When that august organization's Mr Forder asked me into his office, offered me £450 (no mean sum for an author) and the chance to spend a week at Oxburgh Hall during its closed season, I needed no further encouragement.

You see, I cannot abide superstition; the so-called 'paranormal' is, in my humble opinion, nothing more than clutter. Pointless mental clutter.

And yet, as I learnt when arriving here by taxi from Downham Market station, these ancient fears persist.

The taxi-driver, having accepted my fare, cast one glance at Oxburgh Hall, with its dim lantern hanging outside the gatehouse, a pale, wintry moon glinting on the moat, and shuddered. 'You wouldn't catch me staying there, mate,' he muttered. 'Talk about a spooky atmosphere.' And before I could point out that, without an atmosphere (i.e. the gaseous envelope of oxygen and nitrogen around Planet Earth), we would all be in trouble, he had driven off, leaving me alone, my suitcase beside me, outside the great house.

Whistling, I crossed the small bridge to the gatehouse where I found, by the porter's lodge, a small doorbell. I pressed, and a distant tintinnabulation could be heard from the dark recesses of Oxburgh Hall.

No lights came on. There were no distant footsteps from within the house, nothing to break the unearthly silence – not even (I jest) the sound of vampiric bats unfolding! I pressed the bell again, and waited.

After a couple of minutes, I left my suitcase by the gatehouse and wandered into the courtyard. By now my eyes were accustomed to the darkness, and for a moment I took in the magnificence of the house which, illuminated by the moonlight, surrounded me. Even to one normally blind to architectural beauty (my family accuses me of being 'artistically impaired'), the Hall was an astonishing sight.

For five centuries these buildings had belonged to the Bedingfeld family, apart from a brief period in the eighteenth century when the house had been occupied by a Sir Edmund and Lady Challoner. It was around certain unhappy domestic events during these years that a wild vampiric mythology had grown.

'Mr Blacker?'

The voice, from behind me, interrupted my thoughts. I turned quickly, startled that someone could have appeared at the gatehouse without my hearing his approach. Standing by the door was a tall, broad figure, holding my suitcase.

'Apologies,' he said, in a voice that seemed somehow too frail and reedy for his size. 'I was in my room in the East Wing.'

I stepped forward and introduced myself.

'I'm Gilbert Franck,' he said. 'National Trust caretaker.'

'I'm relieved to see you, Mr Franck.' I smiled. 'For a moment I thought I'd been abandoned to the vampires of Oxburgh.'

Laughing, we entered the Hall by a small door to the left of the gatehouse. As he led me up some winding stairs, it occurred to me that the reason why stories had spread of a supernatural presence at the Hall lay in the peace (gloom would be too strong a word) of the building itself. We made our way down a corridor before Franck opened a door, announcing, almost like an old-fashioned butler, 'Your room, Mr Blacker.'

The bedroom in which I now stood was neither grand nor baronial, but a homely little affair with a low, sloping ceiling and a small window overlooking the moat and garden. It had once been a nursery, Franck informed me.

'I shall be serving dinner within fifteen minutes,' Franck said. 'You'll find the dining-room across the courtyard beyond the gatehouse.'

'Dinner? Nothing elaborate, I hope.'

'I like to cook.'

He certainly did. To my pleasure and astonishment, I was treated to a three-course meal by candlelight in the panelled dining-room.

As I partook of the excellent vegetable soup, Franck revealed that he had indeed once been a chef. Since his retirement, the Trust had employed him part-time to look after properties during the closed season.

'Retirement?' I looked up from my soup. 'Forgive me, but you seem rather young to retire.'

Franck inclined his head graciously. 'I'm older than I look,' he said. 'And unfortunately I have a rather delicate heart. My doctor advised me to escape the hurly-burly of the kitchen in favour of a less stressful occupation.'

I observed with a smile that he had lost none of his culinary skills.

He gave a modest shrug, like a man uneasy with compliments. 'Presumably you'll be concentrating on the story of Margaret Challoner,' he asked.

'Yes. A week among the private papers, and I'll be able to put the famous vampires to rest for good and all.'

'You seem remarkably confident, Mr Blacker.'

'Of course I'm confident. You see, demystifying the so-called "paranormal" is something of a hobby of mine. I've already proved to my satisfaction that the original werewolves were nothing more than hungry wolves who were seen by gullible villagers digging up graves for food. As for all those stories about "ghosts" arising from graveyards, it's clear to me that they were simply the bacterial glow – *protobacterium fisheri*, it's called – produced by the decomposing flesh of corpses. Of course, vampires are rather more complex . . .'

So, as I was served my main course – some marvellous poultry dish – I expatiated upon my latest theory.

The myth of the vampire, or *vrykolaka* as it was known in Romania, dated back to the plague. At that time, there was naturally an almost hysterical fear of death. Stories of ghosts tormenting entire villages. Bodies were disinterred, examined. And what was found? Sometimes there was blood around the corpse's mouth. Its flesh seemed alive. When cut, blood still flowed.

'And science has an explanation for all these phenomena?' asked Franck.

I smiled. 'Of course it has. Victims of the pneunomic form of the plague frequently bled around the mouth after death. As the lungs and viscera of the body expanded, blood was forced upwards towards the mouth. In the cases of sudden deaths – which were said to have caused vampirism – the abrupt removal of oxygen from the bloodstream frequently meant that it wouldn't coagulate after death. Hence the running-blood theory.'

'What about the fangs and the long black cloak?' Franck stood up and filled my glass with wine. 'What about red-eyed creatures feasting on the jugular?'

'Funnily enough, traditional vampires were always said to feast on the heart,' I said. 'It was Bram Stoker whose feverish imagination dreamt up the fangs and the neck idea. Before Count Dracula, the folkloric vampire was thought to be a bloated, ruddy-cheeked individual – a putrescent, walking corpse in other words.'

Through my discourse, Gilbert Franck had listened politely but now he winced queasily.

'How is the swan?' he asked.

'Swan?'

'I cooked swan for you tonight.'

I laughed appreciatively. Teachers and critics have been kind enough to comment on the 'humour' of my stories, and I was glad to find that the caretaker was no stranger to zaniness himself. 'Yes, the *swan* was excellent, thank you very much.'

Later, well-fed but tired, I made my way across the courtyard and upstairs, having bid my host a very good night.

So this was a haunted house! To tell the truth, I had rarely felt more at home. Why, even the bed into which I slipped seemed warm and welcoming.

Only once that night was my rest disturbed. Some time in the early hours, I was awoken by a soft weight upon my chest. It appeared that a house cat had adopted me. I smiled in the darkness before drifting off into the deepest of slumbers.

The sleep of the dead, you might say.

No research can have been accomplished in such agreeable circumstances as was mine during the first part of my week at Oxburgh Hall. Rising at eight, I would be treated to one of Gilbert Franck's superb cooked breakfasts. Then to the library for a morning amongst the family papers. Light lunch in the Saloon, more work, a brief constitutional around the garden, and a final session in the library. The day would end with a candlelit meal, with the excellent Franck waiting in attendance.

It is no exaggeration to say that quite soon I had begun to feel as at home as any lord of Oxburgh Hall might have done. In fact, such was my natural authority that Franck had taken to calling me 'sir' and generally behaving as if he were my faithful servant.

I did not correct him – indeed I'm ashamed to say that I discovered I have a taste for being in authority and was rather good at it!

My research, too, was most satisfactory.

The years from which the vampire myth had originated were – perhaps unsurprisingly – ill-documented in the Bedingfeld family papers, but fortunately a local rector, the Reverend Herbert Radcliffe, had recorded events of that time in his diary.

Grief-stricken by the death of his young wife Mary, the fourth baronet Sir Richard Bedingfeld had, in 1767, sent his son to London to be educated by nuns and had himself entered a monastery to become a virtual recluse for the next five years. During that time, according to Radcliffe, a man called Sir Edmund Challoner, a merchant and fellow Catholic, had been allowed to use the house. Challoner spent most of his time in Norwich, leaving his wife Margaret ('a miracle of young comeliness, as spry and gay as a sparrow,' said Radcliffe) at Oxburgh Hall with their young son Edward.

This, it transpired, had been unwise. In 1769, Radcliffe's diary reported 'a tragick vexation at the Hall'.

For some months, there had been noisome rumours in the village, viz. that her ladyship had developed an unseemly affection for Joseph Spiers, a member of the household retinue. Often were the times, according to loose tongues, that her ladyship released her servants from their duties early in the evening, leaving her alone with Spiers and her son, the young Edward. Further improprieties, which it will not be beyond the wit of my readers to imagine, were imputed by local gossips to the young couple.

Whether the word of such outrages reached the ear of Sir Edmund I know not, but the facts of his unhappy discovery are as clear as water. On the night of January 13th of this year, he returned unannounced to Oxburgh Hall to find his wife and Spiers at sport in the Great Hall. Overcome by an intemperate rage – my hand hesitates to record such enormities for posterity – Sir Edmund seized a carving knife from a table nearby and slayed the unhappy couple.

The tragedy was not yet over. The following morning, servants found Sir Edmund hanging by the neck from a rope attached to a beam in the Great Hall. Wandering amidst this unhappy scene was the poor little Edward, no more than nine years of age, so distracted with grief and confusion that he was struck quite dumb.

A messenger brought me post haste to the house where, the bodies having been made decent and laid out in a ground-floor bedchamber,

I pronounced the Office of the Dead upon the three of them.

While we were thus occupied, Edward was seen to walk in a trance out of the house. His body – the final horror – was found in the moat, face down, staring into the murky depths of the water and, I fancy, of the human heart.

God rest their unhappy souls.

'Would you care for some tea, sir?'

I looked up from Radcliffe's diaries to find Gilbert Franck standing before me. I had been so absorbed in the Reverend's account that I had failed to hear him approaching.

'So that was why Sir Richard destroyed the Great Hall,' I said quietly.

'It's possible, sir. No other explanations have been offered for such a drastic step.'

I shivered. 'It's quite a story.'

'A true story, sir.'

'Yes, of course. All fact.' I closed the book and stood up. 'Fact is always somehow more disturbing than fiction.'

And I *was* disturbed. After tea, I walked by the moat, turning over in my mind the details of the Reverend Radcliffe's account. So deep in thought was I that I soon found myself by the small chantry chapel, which was almost concealed by trees on the far side of the drive. It was from there, as the evening gloom closed in on me, that I heard the sound of a human voice, female, singing quietly.

Approaching stealthily, I saw, seated upon a small stone tomb, a woman, dressed in a long, blue velvet dress. As she sang some kind of lullaby to herself, she swayed backwards and forwards, almost like the trees buffeted by the November wind.

From my vantage point on the gravel drive, I could just see that the woman was working on some kind of tapestry. Quite suddenly, as if some- one had called her, she stopped singing. Slowly, she turned to me, gazing through the trees. That face, those features: they weren't pale and sad, as somehow I had been expecting, but almost comically dappled and rosy- cheeked.

She smiled, and the look she gave me was of such heart-stopping inti- macy, such warmth, that, never having been what they call 'a ladies' man', I found myself blushing. Without a word, I hurried back towards the house.

Franck was laying the table in the dining-room.

'There's a woman by the chapel,' I said, rather more loudly than I intended. 'Knitting, singing. In the dark.'

'That would be Miss Preston, sir,' said Franck.

'Miss Preston?' I said angrily. 'Who the hell is Miss Preston, and what is she doing on my – in the grounds?'

'A nanny, sir. She lives in a cottage in the village. Retired.' Something approaching a smile appeared on the caretaker's face. 'You weren't think- ing she was from . . . another place, sir?'

'Certainly not. It was just that, after reading all about the Challoners, it gave me a bit of a turn.'

'Of course, sir.'

I returned to the library, where Franck had thoughtfully lit a fire. I felt rather strange, with that peculiar heaviness that sometimes precedes a bout of flu. Sighing, I returned to my research.

On the fifth day of September I was considerably discomfited by a deputation of three servants from the Hall, requesting upon my doorstep that I should use my sacred offices to rid the great house of what they called 'the curse of vampyres'. In vain I argued with them that the work of the Lord's servant does not extend to the removal of imaginary hobgoblins, particularly from a Catholic household, and that this story was an insult to reason itself.

Yet their perturbation was so great that, out of sheer pastoral sympathy, I was obliged to listen to them as they told their tales of the vampyric presence of Joshua Spiers and Lady Challoner who now, they averred, held Oxburgh Hall in their devilish thrall. Sir Richard Bedingfeld, the servants said, had already succumbed, as had other members of the household. I was solemnly informed that, because no vampyre is invested with a knowledge of his own state, the afflicted continue to believe that they are normal members of the human race.

These then were their fancies. A week later, I called at the Hall during my tour of the parish. There I was told, by one of the very manservants who had visited me the previous week, that all was well and that my services were no longer required.

Such are the strange byways of superstition among servant folk.

I leafed through the rest of Radcliffe diaries, but there were no further mentions of 'vampyres' or indeed of Oxburgh Hall.

Slowly, I laid the book back on the desk. Joshua Spiers and Margaret Challoner. *Because no vampyre is invested with a knowledge of his own state, the afflicted continue to believe that they are normal members of the human race.* I walked out of the library to the West Staircase, where portraits of the family are to be found. All are named, except one. The fifth painting along is of a young woman, described in the guidebook as 'A Lady in Blue, unidentified'. Slim, pale, she was much smaller than the figure I had seen by the chapel, but there was something in those eyes. The blue dress was identical.

Back in the library, I found a book of household accounts. I turned to the year 1769. There, in the list of 'manservants and maidservants' was the name which confirmed Radcliffe's account of the murders.

Joshua Spiers, Cook.

My limbs heavy from the approaching fever, I made my way out of the library towards the kitchen from where I could hear the sound of Franck preparing my evening meal.

'Sir?' The caretaker was standing at the kitchen table, basting what appeared to be a roast sucking pig. 'Is something wrong?' His voice betrayed the mild disapproval of a servant whose territory has been encroached upon.

'A strange coincidence,' I said, in as natural a voice as I could manage. 'The lover of Lady Challoner was, like you, a cook. Funny, that. Something else. Near where little Edward Challoner drowned, I just happened to see a woman, singing to herself in the twilight. A lady in blue, unidentified.'

Franck fixed me with those dark, expressionless eyes. 'I fear you have lost me, sir,' he said quietly.

'If I were the sort of person to believe in vampires – *which I am not* – I might be tempted to reach the conclusion that Joshua Spiers and Margaret Challoner were here, still alive, singing and –' my teeth chattered '– cooking my supper.'

'But that wouldn't be fact, sir. That would be hocus-pocus.'

'Precisely!' I said angrily. 'This is all a stunt, isn't it? The National Trust is so desperate for tourists that it has set up little vampire games to fool the writers of its infernal books. It's . . . it's a scandal.'

'May I venture to suggest that you are not well, sir.'

'Yes, Franck. I have made up my mind. I shall not complete this commission.' I glanced at my watch. It was five-thirty. 'In fact, I shall ring the National Trust right now and tell them of my decision.'

I returned to the Saloon. As luck would have it, Forder was at his desk. He expressed concern for me in my flu-ridden state. Of course he understood if I had lost my enthusiasm for the commission. No, he wouldn't dream of allowing me to return to London by train, feverish and distressed as I was. In fact, he would drive down himself and collect me that very night. Would nine-thirty be acceptable?

It would.

In no condition to eat a meal, I tottered miserably back to my room and packed my case. I sat on my bed, exhausted by this exercise, and waited.

Suddenly the drowsiness which I had felt all day closed in on me as surely as the darkness outside the window. I lay back on the bed and shut my eyes.

When I awoke, it was with a start. I discovered, as I tried to sit up, that sleep had done nothing to ameliorate my fever. Looking at my watch, I cursed. Ten o'clock. Where the hell was Forder? Why hadn't I been awoken?

Unsteadily, I made my way downstairs. A low murmuring sound reached me from the direction of the dining-room. Thank God. The National Trust man must have arrived and, out of politeness, had refrained from . . .

A strange and singular sight awaited me in the dining-room. At the table, seated close together, their features lit by candlelight, were two figures, one dressed in black and one in blue. Gilbert Franck and the woman I had seen outside, Miss Preston.

As I stood, swaying, at the door, they looked at me in silence. Then, in a voice that was somehow less respectful than I had come to expect, Franck said, 'It seemed a shame to waste the sucking pig. Since you were indisposed, I invited Miss Preston for supper.'

'I f-feel terrible. Where's Forder? He's late.'

'Ah. Mr Forder rang, sir. He has been unavoidably detained. He will collect you tomorrow.'

'No.' My legs felt weak and for a moment I felt as if I were about to lose consciousness.

'My lord –' The woman spoke for the first time. She seemed concerned on my behalf but, as she made to stand up, Franck took her hand.

My *lord*? Why did she call me that?

And there, there in the guttering candlelight of the dining-room, I looked and I saw. Two hands, one holding the other, both plump, soft, ruddy. In the swirling mists of semi-consciousness, I suddenly knew with terrifying certainty that this was no stunt. Before me stood the revenant forms of Joshua Spiers and Margaret Challoner, swollen, corpse-like vampires. And me? Why, it was obvious: I was their lord, Sir Edmund Challoner, doomed to act out my own death, trapped by – trapped by what?

'Forder.' My own voice seemed distant, as if it belonged to someone else speaking in another room. 'It was Forder who was so keen that I should come to Oxburgh Hall.' I tried to visualize the man from the Trust. Big, yes, rosy-cheeked – but then all the people I had seen at the National Trust seemed in my mind's eye to have a strange, bloated quality to them.

'Not the whole National Trust, surely?' It was a whisper, almost a death rattle in my throat. 'They can't all be vampires. Not the head of publications. Not the chairman. Not –' my head spun at the horror of it all 'not their patron, Her Majesty –'

'Bedtime, sir.' Franck was standing now. 'Perhaps I could bring you a hot –'

'*No!*' I backed away from the two of them, stumbling out into the courtyard, the sound of my sobbing breath roaring in my ears. I took the first steps on the stairs and stopped, suddenly aware that there was someone standing before me.

'Please, sir.'

It was a child, a boy of nine or ten, dressed in a long, flowing nightgown. He seemed to be trying to tell me something, repeating, with a kind of hopeless desperation, the same phrase.

'Please, sir . . . Please, sir . . .'

'What d'you want?' I asked faintly.

'Please, sir.'

'Who are you?'

It was then I noticed that the child's garment was wet through. He spoke more slowly now, as if the very life of him was ebbing away.

'Flee, sir.' Yes, that was what he was saying. It was a warning. 'Flee –' And, as if he were a dream, a nightmare vision, the child was no longer there.

I was deathly tired. Up the stairs. The bedroom. Lock the door. Out of my clothes. The relief of those warm, welcoming sheets. Sleep.

And, yes, a certain comfort. As usual, I was half-woken by the cat alighting on my stomach. I sighed.

But it was not the sound of my own breath I heard. Like the whispering of the wind through the trees outside, it was the voice of a child.

Flee, sir.

I opened my eyes to look down on the shape that was lying on me.
'My *lord*.'

When it looked up, what I had thought was a cat had the face of a woman, her smiling mouth smeared with blood, her hair clogged and matted. My chest, upon which she rested, was bare. Beside my heart were two neat wounds.

'Margaret, why?' I said, feeling no fear now, only an unbearable sense of loss, of betrayal. 'Why?'

And my voice became a long, peaceful sigh as I felt myself falling into a swoon of silence, and down, down into the sweetest and deepest of sleeps.

I am a man of fact and I have tried to record, as factually as I am able, the extraordinary 'paranormal' fantasy that the combination of my research and a nasty bout of flu inflicted upon me. I am only grateful that my natural common sense has allowed me to put the weird mental aberrations caused by a temporary fever in their proper context.

Today, thank heavens, I am well again. Mr Forder's mission to 'rescue' me has been cancelled. Within two days, as I have told you, I fully expect to have delivered the final fatal stake to the heart of the vampire myth.

Gilbert and Maggie (a new friend, despite being the creature of my weirdest fantasy) now eat with me of an evening. Indeed the meals that Gilbert prepares are of such magnificence that I find I am dramatically gaining weight – to the extent that, as I write, my body tugs at the buttons of my shirt and the very hand with which I write this report seems to swell before my eyes.

I fear that a diet may be ordained when I return home to resume my career, writing books and visiting schools. I can hardly wait to tell my young audiences about the triumph of fact at Oxburgh Hall.

Gather round, children, I shall say. This morning I shall explain to you why there is no such thing as a vampire.

THE DEMON DRUMMER

JAMILA GAVIN

The link between the Demon Drummer and Mompesson House in Salisbury, Wiltshire was slight. There was only the name – and reports of people experiencing 'a presence' in the Green Room. What clinched it for me was the discovery of a drummer boy's badge 300 years later . . .

> No sword, nor rope, nor witch's fire
> Can cause a demon to expire.

Tum tiddly um pom pom. . . . Tum tiddly um pom pom . . . Down the moonlit road came the demon; across the great white plain, where many a ghostly legion had marched – following a drum beat on and on into eternity. 'I want a drum, I want a drum . . . ,' the demon cried. 'Tum tiddly um tum. Tum tiddly dee . . . When I get my drum, you'll follow me!'

It was the sound of the drum which drew the demon to the drummer boy. How smart the lad looked in his scarlet uniform, with yellow sash and blue stockings and the round, shining brass badge pinned to his floppy hat. But it was not the uniform the demon coveted, it was the drum which was strapped across the boy's chest and rested on his left hip, below his heart.

> 'It's not your soul that I require,
> Your drum is all that I desire.'

137

He was new to the regiment, the boy; and so, hour after hour, he practised his drumming, learning to beat the advance, the charge, the retreat, the Roundheads and Cuckolds – and all the points of war.

The drumsticks twirled in his fingers as his beat became sharper and more skilful; volleys of rat tat tat, as piercing as gunfire, echoed round the barracks and were carried high on the winds, which swept across Salisbury Plain; and soldiers smiled to see the young lad strutting about, anticipating the day when he would lead the troops into battle.

But there were those who sighed too, for they knew that the young drummer boys who marched ahead, rapping out the fearful heartbeat of every soldier, were the ones the enemy liked to cut down first – to silence that pulse and make their foe feel that they were dead already.

The demon hung about watching and waiting. He heard another rhythm hammering through his dreadful being. 'I want that drum . . . I want that drum . . . I want that drum . . .'

The demon didn't have long to wait. It was a time of civil war; of uprisings and skirmishes between Royalist and Roundhead. Small armies were being rallied all the time. The Mompessons of Wiltshire were all for the king. Thomas the Younger and his cousin, John, galloped round the villages and towns, recruiting men to fight for Charles against the Parliamentarians.

The drummer boy practised even harder – and when a few dozen men, with barely uniform or boots to replace their farming smocks and mud-caked clogs, set forth with a miscellany of rifles and pistols, hayforks and staves – and not much else to engender confidence, except the fierce, heartbeat drumming of the drummer boy – the demon followed.

'Forward, lads!' bellowed Thomas Mompesson from the lofty heights of his battle horse. 'God save the King!' yelled John Mompesson.

'God save the King,' echoed along the lanes as Royalists came out to cheer, though it seemed utter folly. How could such a raggle taggle of men hope to defy the disciplined troops of Cromwell's soldiers? But they waved and shouted words of encouragement just the same, and the young drummer boy broadened his shoulders with pride and beat a brisk pace, while the demon marched alongside, longing for the moment when it would be he who beat the drum.

They marched across the high plains of Wiltshire and joined up with the forces of John Penruddock – as much a ragged band as they were – and the drums rattled out above the sounds of horses' hooves and clashing swords and the heavy tramp tramp of soldiers' feet.

The battle was a fiasco. Cromwell's Model Army cut them down like ripe corn. Survivors swore they saw the drummer boy fall early on, yet somehow the drum never ceased to beat that day. It beat and beat, even though scores lay dead and wounded. It beat like one demented, when the leaders of the uprising, Penruddock and Grove, were captured and hung, and when Thomas Mompesson and the others fled into hiding.

Somehow that drum never ceased beating; even though the little drummer boy's soul had gone straight to heaven; even though the war was long over and Charles the Second was restored to the throne and all those men had long since laid down their arms and gone back to their farms.

Thomas and John Mompesson had returned to live in Tidworth;

Thomas, to become a Member of Parliament and John, a magistrate; yet the frantic drumming they heard as they had scattered in disarray after that last battle haunted their dreams. John swore he could hear the drum beating even by day, throbbing like blood pumping through veins. The drumming was so real and so persistent; it was as if someone marched up and down outside his house practising. Mrs Mompesson worried about her husband. The war had changed him. Sometimes he seemed deranged, the way he would leap to his feet with wild eyes and shout, 'There it is again – that infernal drumming!'

Many a time he sent out a servant to drive the drummer away, but there was never anybody there.

Then one day, it was louder and closer than usual, and giving way to agitated frustration, John Mompesson rushed out himself and demanded to know who was annoying the neighbourhood hour by hour, day after day, disturbing the peace.

There, in the road outside his house, he saw a strange scarecrow of a boy. Shreds of uniform hung about him – the Royalist colours, it's true – but so tattered that they were almost a mockery to the Crown. However, the drum, which was strapped to his left hip, was a true military drum: taut cream calf's skin was stretched across the top and base and tensioned by white-painted rope, which criss-crossed round the blue, wooden body of the drum. The royal insignia, emblazoned in gold, glowed between the thin, wavy red and white lines which encircled the top beneath the rim.

The drummer's brass badge flared in the sunlight.

'Who are you? And by what authority do you drum in this neighbourhood?'

Was it the sun's reflection which made the boy's eyes glint red, as he mockingly returned the gaze of the angry magistrate?

'Why sir,' he wheedled, 'Here is my warrant.' He pulled forth a half-torn document and held it out for inspection. 'I have the authority,' he said with the hint of a sneer in his voice.

'You'll come with me,' ordered Mompesson. 'I want the bailiff to verify this,' and he marched the vagrant drummer to the bailiff's office.

The bailiff examined the warrant, holding it first right up to his eyes to gaze at it through his pince-nez, then out at arm's length, because he had become long-sighted with age. Then he stared at the pitiful spectacle of the lad before him – was he human? He could hardly contain a shudder, for he looked like some wild creature out of a ditch, with his unkempt hair and filthy hands and the smell about him of something putrid and evil. Yet, there was no denying that the boy was a skilful drummer who knew all the calls and whose shining drum would pass even the closest scrutiny on the king's parade.

'This warrant is obviously a forgery,' declared the bailiff finally, and to the satisfaction of Mr Mompesson, he not only tore it up, but ordered the boy to be arrested and his drum confiscated. The charges, they told him, could be extremely serious; anything ranging from forgery and disturbing the peace, to masquerading as a drummer in the king's uniform and robbing from the dead – for how else had he come into possession of the drum? The penalty could be transportation or death.

The howls and curses of the boy rent the air as they stripped him of the drum. His fingers clawed at it. 'It's mine, it's mine!' he shrieked. 'You cannot deprive me of my property. That drum is mine!' And he cursed and howled like the devil himself, as they dragged it off his body and tore the remnants of uniform from his back.

A constable was summoned to take the fraudulent drummer boy to the town gaol and the bailiff took the drum and locked it away.

'At last,' thought Mr Mompesson. 'I am free of the drumming.'

For a while, Mr Mompesson went cheerily about his business, until one day he was called to London. On that same day, a man came round from the bailiff with the drum which had been confiscated from the vagrant drummer boy.

'The bailiff said that you were to have it, sir,' said the man. 'The drum is now yours.'

Mr Mompesson looked at the drum. For some reason, his heart missed a beat. 'What happened to the vagrant who caused all the nuisance?' he asked. But the man was vague. 'Why sir, did you not yourself have him transported?'

'Ha, ha, ha.' Mompesson thought he heard laughter.

It matters not to a demon whether he be transported or hanged at the crossroads. He can just laugh, and come back again and again – especially if he wants something!

A sudden, fierce wind seemed to taunt the weathervane and send it spinning round, and strange words moaned in his ears:

'It's not your soul that I require
But just the drum that I desire.'

John Mompesson shuddered. The man was holding the wretched drum out to him. He didn't want the thing, but the man pressed it into his hands. As he took possession of it, it gave a hollow echo as Mompesson handed it rapidly to his servant to take indoors. Then he set off for London, saying he would be home the next day.

That night, when the servants had finally locked and bolted the doors of the Mompesson household; when they had dined and cleared away and settled the fires; when the dogs of the house had either stretched out in front of the glowing embers or padded up to the children's bedrooms; when Mrs Mompesson was deeply asleep in her bedchamber – there came a low rattling. It was as if someone was trying the doors at the front of the house. Mrs Mompesson woke briefly, listened a few moments, then fell asleep thinking it must be the wind.

Now the sound came again, this time from the back of the house. Young Barbara, the daughter, awoke. Tap, tap, tap . . . was someone knocking to get in? She sat up curiously. Rappatap tap . . . Rappatap tap . . . A low flame flickered in her bedroom fireplace, casting giant shadows up the walls. 'Who is it?' she whispered. Rat . . . tat . . . tat. The great hound lying on her bed across her legs, who normally would have been the first to leap up with his hair all standing on end, didn't even stir.

The noise got louder and more persistent. First the knocking was on the downstairs back door, but then it came to strike at her windows, where it rapped and rattled so fiercely, that she was sure the panes would break. The girl leapt from her bed with a shriek and ran sobbing to her mother that someone was trying to get into her bedroom. At that moment, her brother Charles also came rushing in, hollering that they were being attacked.

Mrs Mompesson bundled the terrified children into her bed; then she lit the candles, put on her dressing gown and slippers and taking one of the candlesticks, went on to the landing. The knocking and banging seemed to be all round the house – at first, a rhythmic noise, as if someone rapped out a sequence, but then it turned into such a furious hammering, that it was as if the house had been plunged into the very centre of a battle.

The servants came running – white-faced maids from upstairs and half-dressed grooms from the stables. They carried sticks and clubs and crowded together as if prepared for a whole gang of ruffians breaking in. But, although the banging and crashing went on all night, nobody gained entrance, and Mrs Mompesson thanked God for their stout oak doors.

No one got any sleep that night.

When Mr Mompesson got back home, what a tale he had related to him, from every member of the family and then again from the servants. How the house had been attacked – by probably half a dozen or more villains, but who had failed to gain entry.

'Well, I daresay, if they didn't get in last night, we won't be hearing from them again,' soothed Mr Mompesson, though he went round the house and stables with his servants, checking every door and window to see that they were secure.

But the next night, it happened again. At first a wind seemed to sweep round the house so powerfully that the windows jiggled in their frames, and a high-pitched whistling came down the chimneys and pierced their ear-drums where they lay in their beds. Then came the knocking, the same as before. Ratta tat tat . . . ratta tat tat . . . ratta tat tat . . . The rapping went from door to door all around the outside of the house, getting louder and louder like a giant drum preparing the troops for battle.

'Do you hear?' Mrs Mompesson clutched her husband's arm. 'It's the same noise. The villains have come back.'

'I'll soon deal with this,' roared Mr Mompesson, furious at having his household terrorized in this way. With Mrs Mompesson hovering at his side with lighted candelabra, he dragged on his boots, flung a cloak across his back, and then taking up his brace of pistols, thudded downstairs yelling for the male servants, Harry and George.

Harry and George had already been awoken by the banging, and soon appeared, bearing great clubs in their hands. Wide-eyed and afraid, they looked to Mr Mompesson for instructions.

'Open the door, man!' Mr Mompesson ordered George. George pulled down the great iron bolts, and lifted the wooden bar from across the door frame. Then he took one of the huge keys which hung from a near-by hook, and put it into the lock. Before turning it, he paused, fearfully. 'Why not wait till morning, sir,' he quavered. 'There could be a lot of them out there.'

'Don't be such a coward, George. Open it up.'

The huge door swung open. Only the deep void of night met their eyes. The knocking stopped. There was a great silence. Mr Mompesson stepped outside, his pistols cocked, one in each hand, ready to fire. Harry shuffled forward timidly, holding up a burning brand which he had fetched from the fireplace. Two of the dogs, who had been sleeping upstairs, ambled out, stretching and sniffing and wagging their tails. Silently, they followed their master all round the outside of the house while, once again, everything was checked. Mr Mompesson himself tried every door and every window, but all were secure and untouched.

They completed a tour of the grounds and then returned to the front door. 'There's nothing and no one there!' He declared. 'And, what's more, though it's been raining, there isn't a fresh footmark in the mud or any sign of horses or strangers. We're all letting our imaginations run away with us. Look at the dogs! They haven't scented strangers; they don't know what all the fuss is about. It's only the wind!'

But after Mr Mompesson had hustled everyone back to their chambers with reassuring words, he remained downstairs alone, looking suddenly hunched and furtively watchful. He paced up and down, up and down in the hallway, then went and sat at his oak desk in the library, furiously drumming his fingers in a rhythmic tattoo.

He must have slid into the regions of sleep despite himself, for when he suddenly awoke with a jerk, the room swayed with shadows. The candle had burnt right down to a stub, and was wavering around pathetically as it drowned in a pool of wax. Rappatat . . . tat . . . Rappatat . . . tat . . . it was the sound of a drum – yet somehow low and menacing. He knew its parley. It was a drum call to prepare for attack. Mr Mompesson felt a chill of horror creep over his body. Rappatat . . . tat . . . Rappatat . . . tat . . . The sound seemed to be near, yet very, very far away – as if in another world. He got to his feet and grasped his pistols in each hand. He went to the window and looked out. It was not yet dawn. There was no moon, but a strange blue light hovered over the stables. Then he saw him – just briefly; just long enough to recognize the tattered scarlet uniform, the blue stockings and the floppy hat on which the badge gleamed like an evil eye. In his hands, he waved a pair of drumsticks and beat the air in a demonic drum roll.

The shrieks of the vagrant drummer were trapped inside Mr Mompesson's head – the same shrieks the wretched creature had emitted when arrested and deprived of his drum; he heard them again. 'I want my drum . . . I want my drum!'

'No, by God! You won't have it back!' John Mompesson was suddenly overwhelmed with anger.

Some time in the night, Mrs Mompesson heard her husband's footsteps clatter furiously up the staircase, but not to stop at their chamber door. Instead, he carried on to the upper rooms, where the children kept their toys. Now she heard his footsteps pacing relentlessly above her head. 'Mr Mompesson,' she went to the bottom of the stairs and called up nervously, 'Won't you retire now and get some sleep? The danger seems to be over.'

'No, no!' were all the words he uttered, though she wasn't sure if they were addressed to her.

The next morning, he was found slumped at the nursery table, sleeping with the drum clasped in his arms.

A few nights later, the commotion happened again. Just when the household had fallen asleep, there was a great whooshing sound as if giant objects were being hurled over the house; then the knocking started again, fierce as ever; it went from door to door and now up on to the roof, clattering around on the tiles and rumbling down the chimneys.

The household was plunged into terror. Once again, the servants rushed out of the house and confronted the darkness, and again Mr Mompesson raced up the stairs to the nursery, but would not say why. But he knew then it was more than knocking. He understood the language of the drum beating out the advance, the attack, the instructions to rally, or disperse, or retreat.

Night after night, the same thing happened – and with such malice – for it seemed as though whoever made the noise, knew the exact moment that the household had dropped into a deep sleep, and would start up the racket all over again, sending the children into hysterics and bringing dread, fatigue and confusion to the household.

Rappatat tat . . . rappatat . . . tat. . . .

'Dammit, you shan't have it,' muttered Mr Mompesson one night, tossing about as if in the middle of a nightmare.

'Have what, sir?' exclaimed his wife, bewildered.

'The drum. The wretched fellow wants his drum. But he shan't have it,' and he flung himself from his bed and stumbled up to the nursery.

When the banging and crashing and furious commotion was done with, it was the deliberate ratta tat tat of a drummer breaking up the guard, which was always the sinister finale. Only then would Mr Mompesson emerge from the upper room looking white and exhausted.

'Won't you take us away from here, sir?' pleaded his wife.

'There's been no harm done,' said Mr Mompesson coldly. 'No property has been damaged and no person hurt. I will not be harassed and driven out by any damned spirit of the night.'

'But what about my nerves?' wailed poor Mrs Mompesson, utterly distraught, for she was soon to be delivered of another child.

What is it that can make noises so loud they can be heard across the fields, yet the dogs don't stir? What is it that can pant like a hound, move like a cat, be hot without a fire, ride a horse till lame without it even leaving the stable? What hammers without an anvil and snips without scissors? What can throw furniture about, lift children from their beds and rip up a bible? Who drums against the doors and windows night after night, always ending with the breaking up of the guard?

People said it was the devil.

'Fetch the priest, I beg you,' cried Mrs Mompesson. 'The house is possessed!'

A priest came and went from room to room throughout the house intoning a prayer of excorcism: 'Oh Child of the Devil and enemy of everything that is good, stop perverting the right way of the Lord. *In nomine patris filii et spiritus sancti*, I command you to leave this house!' For some weeks after that there was silence – but to Mr Mompesson, it was a mocking silence; a taunting silence. His sleep was still restless and disturbed. For him, there was no peace of mind. He knew the drum gleamed in the room above as if waiting to be claimed by the drummer and, late into the night, he could be heard pacing restlessly and climbing the stairs to lock himself into the nursery.

A few weeks passed. There had been no disturbance; no knocking of any kind. Gradually, the household became confident that the priest had rid them of the demon. Mrs Mompesson had given birth safely and was lying in her own chamber, with her infant in its cradle beside her bed, where she could reach out and rock it.

One night, in the dead of night, when the whole house slept deeply, the knocking came again. 'Pou . . . tou . . .pou . . . tou . . . pou . . . tou . . . R.' It was muffled and intimate; it crept into Mrs Mompesson's dreams. 'Pou tou, pou tou . . . R.' Instinctively, she reached out and touched her baby's cheek. It was soft and warm and she felt its steady breath on her hand.

'Pou tou . . . pou . . . tou.'

'Who's there?' called Mrs Mompesson, at last rousing from her sleep. Nobody answered. 'Poutou . . . poutou . . . R . . . poutou . . . poutou . . . R . . .' the knocking was close by. 'Poutoupoutou . . . pou . . . poutoupoutou pou . . .' It was inside the house. It was at her own chamber door. She wanted to lift her baby from its cradle and hold it to her, but a terrible chill froze her into paralysis.

'Poutoupoutou . . . poutoupoutou pou . . . tou . . .' the knocking continued.

'Who's there?' Mrs Mompesson cried in a dread voice. 'Why don't you come in?'

The door remained firmly shut, but the room was suddenly filled with an awful sulphurous smell. The chair in the corner slid forward slowly and the baby's cradle began to rock. Then before the horrified eyes of its mother, invisible hands lifted the sleeping infant. It lifted it into the air . . . higher and higher . . .

'Please . . .' Mrs Mompesson held out her hands in desperate supplication. 'I beseech you. . . .' Slowly, the baby was lowered again, and laid back into its cradle so gently it didn't wake. The cradle rocked.

'In the name of God, who is it? What do you want?' Mrs Mompesson whispered with a shudder.

And a voice answered, 'Nothing with you.' The chair moved back to its place in the corner and the cradle stopped rocking.

One day, the people of Tidworth gathered around to watch the Mompesson family leave. It was a strange day for them all, for none could remember a time when a Mompesson had not lived in their district. It was whispered that the demon drummer had finally driven them out. The whole town knew about the constant happenings in the Mompesson household. Tales abounded about the poltergeist who threw things about and lifted the children from their beds. Most put it down to the drummer boy, who only wanted his drum back. But Mr Mompesson was a stubborn man. He would rather leave, than give in to the vagrant drummer boy.

So several huge carts arrived, and were piled high with furniture and chests and all their goods and chattels – and it was noted that a military drum was among the things which came out of the children's nursery to be loaded on to the cart along with everything else; and finally, the long procession wound its way to Salisbury – to within the very shadow of the cathedral, where Thomas had prepared a house for them in the Close.

Never had a day seemed more exciting for the children. Just to come into a city like Salisbury – all busy and bustling – and the cathedral bells ringing out, and the streets crowded with people and animals and carriages and hawkers and buskers.

And their house, too, was a most pleasing building – unlike their old one, which had been dark and rambling and draughty and filled with such horror. This one was newly built – in the modern style – a mixture of grey limestone and redbrick with sash windows and hipped roofs. Inside, the rooms were light and airy, each with a view either looking out over the Chorister's Green to the Cathedral, or to the gardens at the back with their walks and flower beds. Even though they were now in the middle of a city, yet their new house had such a gentle peacefulness about it, they were sure that not even a demon drummer could disturb this serenity.

Soon all their furniture and belongings found a place throughout the two-storey building and the family happily made themselves at home.

The business with the demon drummer gradually faded like a bad dream.

Two centuries rolled by; the Mompesson family thrived and died out like an old tree and Mompesson House was inhabited in turn by the Longuevilles, the Hayters, the Portmans, the Townsends, and then in 1952, a Mr Martineau moved into Mompesson House.

In a nearby village, a boy was at home for the school holidays.

It was summer half-term. The boy's father, Mr Hammick, had purchased a new car, and so was looking for every opportunity to drive it.

'Fancy a spin, Philip?' he asked his son.

The roads were still empty stretches of grey ribbon, and driving was an entertainment and a sport. Mr Hammick put on his tweed jacket and cap, as if he might have been taking out the trap and pony, but instead, they leapt into his latest passion – a bright red MG sports car with shining chrome grid and side lamps.

They climbed the steep wooded escarpments – richly green, and after winding ever upwards through deep-shadowed tunnels of elm and beech trees, they broke out into the vast open expanse of Salisbury Plain.

At a crossroads, Mr Hammick slowed down to point out a signpost to Tidworth. 'That's where the demon drummer comes from,' he announced.

Philip hardly noticed when they passed the great, grey slabs of Stonehenge, so intent was he on the strange story of the demon drummer of Tidworth, sometimes known as the Mompesson Ghost, which his father then related to him.

'And is he still around?' asked the boy, excitedly.

'They say he left Tidworth when the Mompessons left for Salisbury,' replied his father. 'I used to spend my holidays at Mompesson House in Salisbury, in the days when my Uncle Willie lived there, but I can't say I ever heard or saw a thing. It was most annoying – especially as Annie, the housemaid, swore she felt a "presence" in the Green Room and always whistled "We're Soldiers of the Queen" though she knew not why.'

'Oh!' Philip sighed with disappointment.

'Why don't we go to Salisbury and look at the house? I haven't seen it since I was a boy,' said Mr Hammick with sudden enthusiasm. 'We're so close to it now.'

Soon, the great spire of Salisbury Cathedral rose before them like a finger, powerful yet delicate, pointing upwards into the pale blue sky. They drove right into the Close and parked the car outside the railings of Mompesson House.

Mr Hammick got out – suddenly overwhelmed with memories. He walked up and ran his fingers along the railings, and lovingly looked all over its stone and brick front. 'Look, Philip, the magnolia – it's still there, and blooming as beautifully as ever! They say it's nearly as old as the house!'

'Shall we go in, Father?' asked the boy.

'It would be rather impertinent, since we haven't made an appointment,' murmured his father, though he looked longingly at the great front door, with its elaborately sculpted cartouche of the Mompesson coat of arms. 'Oh, to hell with it. They can't eat us, can they? Let's try.' He lifted the catch of the wrought iron gate, walked up to the door and boldly rang the brass bell.

'Yes?' The man who opened the door viewed them with cool reserve, as if mildly annoyed that he had been disturbed.

'Oh . . . er . . . do forgive us!' stammered Mr Hammick. 'Are you Mr . . . er . . . um. . . .'

'Mr Martineau,' the man informed them.

'Ah! So you're the new owner of Mompesson House, then,' declared Mr Hammick, his enthusiasm overcoming his shyness.

'Yes, can I help you?' Mr Martineau had not yet opened the door a jot further than was sufficient to see who had knocked.

'Forgive me, sir . . .' Mr Hammick apologized again. 'I know this is grossly impertinent of me, but I couldn't resist calling by as we were passing. You see, I visited this house as a child – and I loved it so much.'

'Oh, I see, well – perhaps you'd better step inside.'

With conspicuous reluctance, Mr Martineau stood back and allowed father and son into the hall.

Mr Hammick's eyes roamed eagerly around, taking in again, after so long, the beautiful plasterwork, the delicate mouldings and the collections of masks and ornaments. Finally and irrevocably his gaze settled on the elegant oak staircase leading upwards to rooms at the top in which he had once slept and played as a boy.

For a while they talked, or rather, it was Mr Hammick who mainly reminisced about the house: who had lived there and what they did, what changes had been made, and what changes would be made, till finally, his son, Philip, unable to withhold his curiosity any longer, burst out, 'But please, Mr Martineau, sir! Have you seen or heard the ghost?'

Mr Martineau's smile could scarcely disguise the faint contempt he felt for the question. 'I don't believe in ghosts,' he said primly.

Mr Hammick, who was well away now with his memories, was prompted then to regale Mr Martineau with the story about the Mompesson drummer boy, insisting that, as the new owner of the house, he should at least be familiar with the story, even if the ghost is no more.

At first, Mr Martineau stood politely stony-faced, as Mr Hammick plunged into details of the account, but slowly his face took on an expression of intense interest and by the end, the faintest flush of excitement tinged his cheeks.

'Just one moment,' said Mr Martineau, when the story had finally ended – it had to be admitted – somewhat inconclusively. 'Wait here. I think there is something you might be interested in seeing.'

He rapidly ascended the staircase and entered the Green Room which was at its head.

Soon he reappeared with something clenched in one hand. 'As you can see, I'm in the process of renovating the house, and I've had the electricians in to re-wire it. Yesterday, one of the men had to lift up the floorboards of the Green Room. He found this.'

Mr Martineau opened up his hand. Lying on his palm was a discoloured, dusty brass badge.

'Good Heavens!' Mr Hammick looked absolutely stunned. He took the badge cautiously, almost as if it might burn him. His fingers stroked the embossed brass, and he rubbed it to a shine on the front of his jacket. Then he looked at it again, hardly believing what he saw – the image of a drum with crossed sticks and the Royalist insignia.

'What is it, Pa?' asked Philip.

'It's the badge of a drummer boy!'

They stood silent with astonishment.

Then Mr Martineau spoke stiffly. 'Well, now – if you'll excuse me.' His hand trembled as he held it out to take back the badge. Hardly giving it a further glance, he slipped it into his jacket pocket and then opened the front door.

'I'm afraid I must get on. Perhaps you'll call again another time.' But he spoke without any welcoming warmth, and father and son knew that it would be a long time before either of them would enter that house again.

They drove out of Salisbury, back across the plain, and on past the signpost to Tidworth.

'I wonder what happened to the drum,' murmured the boy.

How pretty the Close looks at night: the elegant houses round the Green, with their tall windows and looped curtains, where glimpses of crystal chandeliers flicker warmly and the shadows of children bob up and down against the walls. And how safe it feels to see the nightwatchman patrolling the Close – and just to live within the embrace of a house of God, whose tall spire reaches up to heaven. Could such a place be touched by evil?

Mrs Mompesson often toured the house at night, after she had tucked in her children. They had found peace at last. No longer were their nights disturbed. The dark rings of exhaustion had faded from beneath their eyes, and their pale cheeks glowed like winter roses.

Tonight, she went into the Green Room. She did this every night, as if for reassurance, for it was here, along with the children's other toys, that

the drum was stored, long ago abandoned by young Charles, who was far more keen on riding his pony.

Placing her candlestick on the table, she gazed out of the window across the Green.

Suddenly, she saw him. A boy; dressed in a scarlet jacket and breeches and sash, and a badge shining on his floppy hat. In his hands he twirled a pair of drumsticks with which he beat the empty air – for he had no drum.

With a dreadful shudder, she realized immediately who it was. The rhythm came hammering into her brain. Rappatat . . . tat . . . rappatat . . . tat . . .

'No,' she whispered. 'Not here, too. Please, not here.'

'I want the drum . . . I want the drum . . .' a voice broke into her thoughts.

Without any hesitation, Mrs Mompesson turned to the far corner table on which rested the drum. Its white ropes hadn't faded, and its body of royal colours gleamed as brightly as if they had just been painted. She picked it up. Her ring struck the calfskin surface and it boomed like a soft heartbeat. She opened the sash window to its maximum, then leaning out, she hurled the drum with all her might – over the wrought iron railings, beyond the walls with the magnolia; over the Green it went, spinning towards the drummer boy. It spun and twirled and somersaulted higher than the cathedral spire, higher and higher till it merged with the multitude of stars – and a great shout of joy echoed among the peal of bells striking midnight.

She heard the ratta . . . tat . . . tat of a drum.

She didn't know it was the beat of the retreat, but she heard it receding into the distance – and soon it was gone for ever.

THE AUTHORS

———————— • ————————

Ted Hughes, the leading British poet, was appointed Poet Laureate in 1984. Several volumes of his verse are intended for children, such as *What is the Truth?* which won the Guardian Children's Fiction Award in 1985, but he has also written many children's stories, including *The Iron Man* and *Nessie the Mannerless Monster*. *The Iron Woman*, his sequel to *The Iron Man*, was published in 1993. Born in Mytholmroyd, West Yorkshire, Ted Hughes now lives in the West Country.

Berlie Doherty worked as a social worker and a teacher before becoming a full-time writer. Born in Liverpool, she now lives in Sheffield and is a member of the Northern Association of Writers in Education and of the advisory committee for Open Learning at BBC Radio Sheffield. Her children's books, many of which have been read on national radio, include *How Green Are You?*, *Granny was a Buffer Girl* – which won the Carnegie Medal – and *Paddiwak and Cosy*.

Michael Morpurgo commissioned the stories for this book, as well as contributing his own chilling tale. He is the author of over forty books for children, four of which have been made into films or television plays, including *Why the Whales Came*. He left his work as a teacher to write, and to set up his charity, Farms for City Children, which he runs with his wife from their home in Devon.

John Quinn, was born in County Meath, Ireland and worked as a teacher before becoming a radio producer in the Education Department of RTE, the Irish Broadcasting Service. He has had three children's books published to date: *Duck and Swan*, *The Gold Cross of Killadoo* and *The Summer of Lily and Esme*. The latter won the Bisto Children's Book of the Year Award in 1992.

Dick King-Smith was a farmer in Gloucestershire for most of his life before launching himself as an author in his late fifties. He has had more than seventy children's stories published, most of them about animals, and his top seller, *The Sheep Pig*, won the Guardian Children's Fiction Award in 1984. He now combines writing with a job as a television presenter, and lives in the West Country with his wife.

Anne Merrick has been writing for children all her life. She attended Nottingham University where she obtained an English Literature degree and met her husband, Brian. Anne has taught in primary, secondary and higher education and is on the committee of Children's Literature in Education. Her first children's novel to be published, *Someone Came Knocking*, was short-listed for the 1994 Carnegie Medal.

Joan Aiken, daughter of the American poet Conrad Aiken, had her first stories published when she was in her late teens. She has written many short stories for children, but her imaginative children's novels, which include such well-known titles as *The Wolves of Willoughby Chase*, *Black Hearts in Battersea* and *Night Birds on Nantucket* established her as a popular and creative writer for children.

Alick Rowe began writing for radio after a highly successful teaching career. His first major serial was *Intimate Strangers*, produced for LWT, followed by four episodes of *The Prime of Miss Jean Brodie* for Scottish Television. His children's novels include *Voices of Danger* and *The Panic Wall*.

Terence Blacker's *Ms Wiz* series of nine children's stories about a highly eccentric modern witch is still as popular as it was in 1988, when the books were first published. He is now creating a new and equally hilarious series, *Hot Shots*, about a girls' football team and is rapidly establishing himself as a top writer in the children's book field. His adult novels are *Fixx* and *The Fame Hotel*.

Jamila Gavin was born in Mussoorie, India of an Indian father and an English mother, and her schooling was divided between the two countries. She considers that she has spent her life trying to belong to both cultures. Her children's novel *The Wheel of Surya* was runner-up for the Guardian Children's Fiction Prize and her other books include *The Singing Bowls* and *Grandpa Chatterji*.

NATIONAL TRUST PROPERTIES
FEATURED IN THE STORIES

———————— • ————————

Hardcastle Crags, West Yorkshire
An area of wooded countryside near Hebden Bridge consisting of two steep valleys, both with streams running through them. There are dramatic rock outcrops (the Crags) in the woods, and riverside walks beside Hebden Water leading to a disused nineteenth-century cotton mill.

Hardy's Cottage, Dorset
A small thatched cottage near Dorchester where Thomas Hardy was born in 1840. The cottage was built by his great-grandfather and has been altered very little in the last century. Every plant mentioned in Hardy's novels is grown in the cottage garden.

National Trust properties in North Devon
The Trust owns several houses in North Devon, including Arlington Court, near Barnstaple with its impressive collection of carriages and Watersmeet House, a fishing lodge near Lynmouth. A great deal of North Devon coast and countryside, including the area around the East Lyn River and Hoar Oak River, is also protected by the Trust.

Coney Island, County Armagh, Northern Ireland
A wooded island on Lough Neagh, right in the centre of Northern Ireland. It was almost certainly once linked to the mainland by a causeway, parts of which still appear above the water. A Neolithic settlement has also been found on the island.

National Trust farms
The Trust owns hundreds of working farms all over the country. There are approximately eighty fell farms in the Lake District alone. At Wimpole Home Farm in Cambridgeshire a fascinating variety of rare breeds of farm animals can be seen, including hens, pigs, cows and sheep; and at Lower Treginnis in Wales the Trust have turned over their farm to become the third 'Farm for City Children'.

Castle Drogo, Devon
This remarkable twentieth-century granite castle, designed by Sir Edwin Lutyens, overlooks the Teign valley. It contains furniture by Lutyens, including the round kitchen table and even some specially designed pastry boards.

Countryside around Malvern, Hereford and Worcester
The National Trust owns over 1,250 acres in the Malvern Hills, comprising Foxhall on the east slope, Midsummer Hill, and the Southern Hills from Little Malvern to Chase End Hills.

Oxburgh Hall, Norfolk
A magnificent moated courtyard house built by the Bedingfeld family in the late Middle Ages. The interior is a mixture of Tudor, neo-classical and Victorian decoration, and visitors can see embroidery worked by Mary Queen of Scots during her captivity.

Mompesson House, Salisbury, Wiltshire
An attractive eighteenth-century house in the cathedral close, built in 1701 for the local Member of Parliament, Charles Mompesson. There is fine plasterwork in several of the rooms, and important collections of porcelain and glass.

PAVILION CLASSICS

published in association with The National Trust

———————— • ————————

THE WIND IN THE WILLOWS
Kenneth Grahame
Illustrated by Graham Percy
The enchanting and amusing adventures
of Toad and his friends Ratty, Mole and
wise old Badger have an ageless quality
which has made this story a firm favourite
with adults and children alike.

THE JUNGLE BOOK
Rudyard Kipling
Paintings by Gregory Alexander
Gregory Alexander's vivid and exotic
paintings of jungle scenes add a new
dimension to the stories of Mowgli and
wild animals of the Indian jungle.

JUST SO STORIES
Rudyard Kipling
Illustrated by Safaya Salter
In this edition, each of the 'best-beloved'
tales is accompanied by a poem by
Kipling, and illustrated with Safaya
Salter's jewel-like paintings which bring a
new magic to the stories.

BLACK BEAUTY
Anna Sewell
Illustrated by Dinah Dryhurst
The moving story of this classic horse is
still one of the best-loved animal
adventures ever written.

THE RAILWAY CHILDREN
Edith Nesbit
Illustrated by Dinah Dryhurst
The thrilling escapades of the three
railway children have been brought to life
in this new edition by Dinah Dryhurst's
fresh watercolour paintings.

ARTHUR, HIGH KING OF BRITAIN
Michael Morpurgo
Illustrated by Michael Foreman
A brilliant modern retelling of the
Arthurian legends, which recreates the
exciting and tragic story of the young king
and his heroic knights of the Round
Table. This classic book is illustrated by
Michael Foreman, who captures the
magic of Camelot and the drama of the
battlefield in vivid colour.

These books can be ordered from the publisher.
Please contact the Marketing Department.
But try your bookshop first.